A NOTE ON THE AUTHOR

Jo Turner grew up in Croydon in South London. After a successful career in journalism, Jo progressed to teaching Modern Languages, English and Media Studies in an East London secondary school. Having been awarded a Master's Degree in Creative Writing at Cambridge University in 2020, Jo went on to complete *Little Spark*, her first novel. She is now working on a sequel, set in Marseille.

ISBN: HB: 978-1-8382595-6-3
ISBN: TPB: 978-1-8382595-5-6
ISBN:eBook: 978-1-8382595-7-0
Compilation & Cover Design by S A Harrison
Published by WriteSideLeft UK
https://www.writesideleft.com

LITTLE SPARK

Jo Turner

write|side|left
2021

For Frank

"But the world is a dark enough place for even a little flicker to be welcome."

Terence Rattigan, *The Deep Blue Sea*

CHAPTER 1

Lake Maggiore, Italy, April 1935

When Eva looks back at the lake, she feels her punishment all over again.

She pauses on the stepping-stones that guide tourists up the dry hill to the church and watches the grey slice of water shimmer through the ornamental palm trees and palazzo parapets. The faint calls of people splashing about in hired rowing boats echo back from the hills behind her.

Eva turns away quickly.

She narrows her eyes to the fierce evening sun and unglues a clump of hair from her damp neck. The town's main church looms wearily above her like a disappointed parent. She does not like this big church, at the top of the hill. And to have to scramble up to it on such a hot day, well, it is typical of her mother to volunteer her for such a thing.

Why couldn't the wake be held in her own little church, at the bottom of the town? Nestling in the cool shadows of the ancient quarter, the little church at least inspires a sense of peace. Every Sunday, sitting next to her mother, she keeps a pious expression as the Padre urges the tiny congregation towards duty, submission and sacrifice. To take her mind off his lofty words, she studies the painting of Saint Roque behind the altar. Painted by a local artist; the 'lake saint' looks thin with bluish skin, at his feet sits a little dog with a cake in its mouth. She always means to ask her mother to tell her the story of the dog, the cake and the saint but, at the end of every service, Paola usually disappears out into the sunlight to share in the congregation's greedy gossip, shouldering her way towards the best nuggets of information like a hungry fledgling. Eva slips away down the street towards home before she overhears Paola talking about her 'unmarried daughter'. Sometimes, Paola does not come home for hours.

While her little church holds no more than thirty people, plenty enough to form a jury on the trials of daughters, this one at the top of the hill must be twenty times its size. It pokes its white tower through the spindly trees as though it, too, would like to cast judgment on the lake below.

Eva sighs, pulls her hessian bag close to her chest, and continues her climb.

At the sound of footsteps she looks up to see three women, coming round the corner at the top of the lane next to the church, ready to descend the hill. As they draw nearer, she hears their chatter. Eva can tell their nationality instantly by their unsuitable clothes and the ornate sun parasols dangling from their wrists.

Eva, who learned English from a poor Devonian artist sharing her tenement house in Milan, cannot understand what these women are saying, mainly because they are all talking at once. But she can tell their disappointment from the slap of their sandals on the paving stones and the slump of their bellies. They seem to be chastising the youngest one for wasting their time on such a climb and such a church. As Eva steps aside to let them pass, smiles spring dutifully to their faces as they recognise the marks of a local girl: the dark heavy dress, the white collar, the black-strapped shoes.

"Buon giorno!" they sing out in their sequence as they stomp down the hill. She longs to tell them that she is not a local, Cannero girl. She did not grow up in this backwater, so she does not have to demonstrate servility to the wealthy travellers of Western Europe.

"Buona sera, signore." She bows her head a little to hide the tiny guilt she feels for the language lesson she is giving them.

"Sorry! Buona *sera*, of course!"

Eva can still hear them giggling their apologies when she reaches the top of the hill and turns at last to face the church. Apart from its whiteness and its bleak, featureless walls, there is nothing impressive about it. It is like a tomb of a vengeful giant, grown ready-made from the dry earth beneath it.

It is no Duomo.

An image of the beautiful young women striding across the square before Milan's pink-stoned cathedral, every inch of their bodies accepting the city's admiration, comes into Eva's mind. At six o'clock in the evening in Milan, she would perch on a shady wall to watch them going to meet their friends and lovers. When will she do that again?

Her mother always says *the future will come regardless*.

Maybe it will. Or maybe it will need a push.

Eva tries to ignore the noticeboard outside the church, which is filled with a large poster for a workers' entertainment taking place in the village. Back in Milan, she grew accustomed to avoiding these tacky displays of power by the fascist regime there. A show of Mussolini's strength in the guise of a free night out for the poor and oppressed. She would rather stay in and sew with her mother, even if it means straining her eyes and hardening her mind to her mother's recriminations.

A noise like a moan draws her attention. A man sits on the bench outside the church, a few metres from Eva. He is hunched over as though this will spare him from the strong sun that beats on his back. His clothes are too heavy for the heat. He takes his head in his hands and rubs his temples, before issuing a purging cry of frustration or pain, or even ensuing sunstroke, which Eva cannot decipher. Then he pulls himself up from the bench, whereupon she sees that he is older than she imagined. He could be forty. His hair flops over his face in the English style, bobbing over his nose as she watches him walk around the back of her to the steps that lead back down to the lake.

Eva watches him take the steps two at a time and then presses her shoulder against the black oak door, which is twice as tall as herself.

As she enters, the cool of the church breathes a sigh over her. She stands a moment, her bag still clasped across her chest as her eyes adjust to the shadows. Eva shivers under the stare of the holy gaze of the saints, poised on plinths as though they would hurl themselves to the ground at the first sign of sin. A willowy Madonna cradles her child selfishly, scowling at the absent congregation. A dark crucifix leans over, way above her head, so high up it hurts her neck to look at it. A pigeon complains in the eaves behind. The evening sun struggles through the lofty windows, greyed with dust, to light up a simple coffin perched before the altar.

Before Eva approaches the coffin, she thinks of Saint Roque's little dog. A devoted servant, she tells herself, always tries to meet the needs of its master, even when its attempts are futile.

Her duty here is futile, too. Nothing will bring this man back to life. She endeavours to suppress the natural aversion, shared by all those living, to witnessing the dead. She must do what is necessary. She has been asked here to prepare this member of God's flock to meet his maker. She scrapes past a pew, startles herself at its screech echoing through the stone rafters.

A door opens at the far end of the church, obscured by the darkness of the confessional box. As the priest emerges Eva turns on a compliant smile. Padre Giacomo is large and round and his cassock is smeared with drops of strong-smelling almond aperitif. He bumps into a few pews on his way towards her. When he sees how young his helper is, he raises his hands in an effort to conceal the stains.

"My child," he gasps, as he approaches her, his breath a smoke of hemlocked alcohol. "You are Signora Mazzanti's child? Yes, I see her eyes, her…"

"I have come to prepare the body." Eva pulls her shawl around herself as his eyes fall below her neck. "What is the name of the deceased?"

He looks over at the coffin and sighs. "First remind me of your name, child."

"It is Eva, Father." She flinches at the word 'child'. So many people seem to regard her as such that she has learned to hide within its unthreatening anonymity. The padre, like all the rest, remains oblivious to her rage.

"And you are prepared to carry out your duty to God on this occasion, Eva? It may be quite… how can I say… distasteful?"

"I am, Father." Eva stares at the stone floor, trying to ignore the priest's spittle collecting at the corner of his mouth.

"That is good, my child." He takes a wheezing breath. "Preparing the dead to meet their maker has always been performed by my young brother Romano up to now, but he has been chosen by God to serve our beloved country and restore Rome to its former glory in the eyes of…" Eva follows the priest's gaze, which has rested on one of the stained glass windows. The coloured glass seems to show a greyhound balanced on top of a bluish globe.

"The world?"

"Yes, exactly, the world. Italy will be great again in the eyes of the world." He focusses his eyes on her with difficulty. "How old are you, my child?"

"I am twenty, father." Now she holds his gaze. Eva believes a Milanesa can stare at whom she likes. She will certainly not look away just for a man, no matter what the authorities dictate.

"Plenty old enough for this task." His voice softens as he looks at her longer. "Also for the more important one of adding to the population of our beloved country, as Il

Duce has requested. Two million lire he has given us in his generosity! For doing what comes naturally!"

Eva shudders. Repopulating Italy is the last thing she wants to do. In Milan, she shunned the advances of the young men who would shout and catcall, huddled around a Moto Guzzi motorcycle, always in a group, as though they were too scared to hunt alone. More fool the girls who gave in to their ugly leering and gesturing. One by one her friends had married, some even having children. As though the Duce gives a damn. All she can see is that the lives of her friends are over before they have begun, although she knows better than to divulge such unpatriotic yearnings to anybody. Even her mother does not know the depth of her feelings. She does not dare to speak of them, not even write of them in her diary. OVRA is everywhere, her mother reminds her, the secret police force ready to pounce on anyone showing such disloyalty to Il Duce. Even in this tiny town, she reminds herself, and smiles. Thankfully, there are not many young men in this place. Just some old fishermen and dusty hoteliers in suits of a bygone era.

"So many young men have left us to serve our country, or to find work in the city," continues Padre Giacomo. "There are hardly enough left behind to service our young women. Hah! We have to rely on the older ones!" The priest puffs out his chest and smooths his cassock over it. "Still, you are new here. You will learn our ways…"

She raises her chin in disgust. The priest takes a step back and his rasping breath returns to a slow wheeze.

"And why did your mother volunteer you to carry out this none too pleasant…?" He waves towards the coffin as though the corpse it contains is no longer even flesh and blood.

"I have prepared bodies for their burials in Milan before." She slows her words, thinking hard. She knows she cannot reveal the real reason why she is doing this. That this is just a practice run for the real thing. It is far too dangerous to divulge the truth to anyone. How she longs to leave Italy and its rigid codes, let alone a wish to work in Hollywood. Within weeks, she could be whisked away to work in a munitions factory somewhere. "I am good with make-up," she says. "I have collected many cosmetics and utensils in Milan. It is easy for me." Eva taps the hessian bag at her chest, and the little bottles and phials sing back. Their music reminds her that, one day, they may buy her a ticket out of this place, even out of Italy altogether.

"I see, child," the priest looks thirstily towards the sacristy. "Well, you have an hour before we have to open the doors for any mourners to come and view the body. Although, who would come to mourn a stranger, I cannot imagine! No identification on him at all — a friendless drunk from over the border is my guess. Commissario Bianchi agrees with me. He has had his likeness taken at the police station, so there are no more formalities to perform. Embalming is hardly necessary, he says... in the circumstances."

"Yes, father." She turns away towards the coffin, tightening her clutch on her bag.

"One other thing, my child!" The priest rests a shaking hand on her arm. "My heart, my chest, they are not good. I need to be resting in bed, the doctors tell me. So I cannot sit up with the body all night, God forgive me. I would therefore request that you carry out this duty on my behalf." He lowers his head and looks up at her through long, feminine eyelashes. "At least until dawn when I will be preparing for early morning *Prime*."

"Yes, father. I have already told my mother not to expect me until after breakfast."

The priest knots his brows and considers her again. "A clever child... An admirable quality, certainly... maybe not in a wife, but admirable nonetheless."

She watches him sway towards the sacristy, follows silently and shuts the door behind him. Then she turns to peer along the length of the gloomy church. She is alone. The smell of the incense, the rotting plaster and wilting flowers is both repellent and comforting. The downcast faces of the saints fix their eyes on her.

Walking towards the coffin, which has been placed on two worm-eaten wooden trestles, Eva hesitates. She has only performed this duty once before in Milan and the prospect of doing it again threatens to overwhelm her. Contemplating the divide between the living and the dead, she finds that it is smaller than she would like.

Eva peers over the edge of the open coffin and into the face of the stranger. He is handsome, around twenty-five, fair-haired, with none of the signs of swift decay that are the hallmark of a watery death. His clothes, a brownish suit of a cheap cotton and pale, lemony shirt, still smell damp. He can't have been out of the water for more than a day.

She has already seen plenty of drowned people on display in this church. Even though she has lived in Cannero less than a year, she knows the lake is the source of most of its dead: some the result of arguments that can no longer be safely had in the public eye without alarming the wrong people. Disputes between neighbours easily escalate when one of the parties wishes to bring it to a swift conclusion, just by writing a note to the Commissario. Others are simple executions, although nobody talks about them, not to Eva, anyway. She had heard of OVRA in Milan, of course. The activities of the Organization for Vigilance and Repression of Anti-Fascism, are notorious, if never discussed, throughout Italy. But here, in Maggiore, they inspire even more fear. It is well known they won't bother to check your identity before they arrest you, or kill you, according to Eva's mother. No amount of make-up can conceal the green tang of their victim's skin or the sunken eye sockets once the heavy body has been dragged from the water.

Eva opens her small cloth bag, takes out a comb and begins drawing it through the man's knotted curls, hair longer than the local Italians tolerate. She has about an hour to complete her work before the local community will be permitted to enter. In accordance with local tradition, the church will stay open all night to welcome any visitors who wish to pay their respects to the dead man.

She puts away the comb in her bag, takes out a little cloth and walks over to the font to moisten it with holy water. As she works, wiping the mud and tiny fragments of weed from his face, Eva finds herself feeling sorrow for the loss of this young man. If she had met him while he lived, would he have been different to all the rest? As she finishes, she hears a quiet whistle coming from the main door of the church, like the soft call of a mermaid. The sound seems to blow itself up the aisle towards her, increasing in intensity so that she can almost see it.

It draws nearer and she closes her eyes. The sound becomes a picture in her mind, so vivid she could reach out and touch it.

A tall man dangles a baby on his knee. She at once knows that the baby is herself. The man bounces her up and down, holding her hands, her bowed legs balancing and bending on his before jumping up into the air in a charade of vertical flight. The baby's face is fixed in concentration at the complexities of the game, while the man laughs quietly on her behalf. Suddenly, he stands, folding her with his slim hands to his chest. He kisses her on the forehead, a kiss that lasts several hissing breaths as he takes in her warm scent, so newly formed as to be almost imperceptible.

Her father.

She has heard the story so many times that it now repeats in her head like a nursery rhyme. How her father went to war, went to war. How he died, how he died. The battlefield is a noble place to die, says her mother, let's hope he was brave.

It has been hard for her mother. Left a widow in a big city with a baby. Her mother's family had drifted off or died out long before she was born and there was no sign of any in-laws on her father's side. Family life was a casualty of war for Eva, and, as a result, she quickly gave her forgiveness when her mother lost her temper. Even now, when her mother is too pleading when looking for buyers for their needlework, sometimes even weeping as she describes how she brought her child up alone, Eva bites her lip.

She opens her eyes and looks into the face of the poor drowned man. Her father would have been about the same age when he died. Would her father have had such soft skin, or laughter lines as playful as these, she wonders? Eva has always known better than to pester Paola about him, for fear of sending her back into what her mother poetically calls *il fondo*: the depths of despair. There is nothing poetic about Paola's silences, which can sometimes last for weeks. Often, Paola disappears for hours during such spells.

Their last conversation on the subject was about two years ago after Eva had come home from school to discover that her mother had sold her wedding ring and sent the money to Il Duce as a contribution towards the coming war in Abyssinia. The argument ended with her mother threatening to throw Eva out if she did not start dressing in the regulation black pinafore that Mussolini insisted Italian minors wore. Eva hated the sight of all those children lined up like soldier ants, and had stopped wearing her own pinafore as soon as it got too tight, but she had never asked for a bigger one. Finally, Eva used a final blow to silence her mother: uniforms only bring misery to people, she cried. Look at Papa.

A few weeks later, her mother had closed up the flat in Milan, and moved herself and Eva, and their few possessions, to the town of Cannero, one of the smaller tourist resorts on Lake Maggiore. We are going somewhere where they will value our craft, Paola had told her daughter. And that was that. Eva tried not to think about that horrible journey — train, bus, another bus and a humiliating walk through an unknown town dragging three suitcases and a hatbox full of embroidery threads, scrutinised by the local inhabitants, who were under no illusion that the new arrivals were any sort of tourist.

The image of her father fading back down the aisle, Eva concentrates on the task in hand. She lays her bag open and lovingly swirls her fingers among her precious compacts, phials and tiny boxes made of stiff card. Every piece has its own history, saved up for and purchased with equal enthusiasm and hope. Their vivid colours and sleek surfaces always bring her a singular joy, even if she is employing them in such a macabre occupation. Their very names are a source of hope: 'Tangee', 'Not Afraid to Kiss' and 'Rouge de la Première Nuit'. She selects a sandy powder, 'Encharma', which will warm his pallid skin. She takes a long brush and begins to apply it gently over his face and neck. One day, she thinks, I will be doing this for Katherine Hepburn and Bette Davis. Then she sees the livid red marks around the man's neck. She draws back for a moment. Has he been strangled? Does he have a grisly story that, even now, will be being repeated in the bars around the lake by the shifty characters who come out after dark? Don't be ridiculous, she tells herself, the reeds are plentiful at the bottom of the lake and are quite capable of causing such damage. She layers the powder over the marks. She sighs again. The water, says her mother, is a violent adversary. Better to keep away.

She decides against the mascara and lip paint that she has witnessed on other grotesque male cadavers prepared by less skillful attendants. His gentle features remind her of the statues she has seen in the Duomo. She sees wisdom, kindness and a deep hurt hidden in the curves of his profile.

She gets up to unlock the main door and kneels down at the front of the church. The vigil begins, but without mourners it feels brittle and false. Still, she is here to commend his soul to the heavens. She begins to pray.

Let these violent times be over.

§

"Buon giorno, signorina."

Deep in slumber, Eva hasn't heard the man enter. His unexpected appearance in the graceless dawn light makes her sit up, now fully alert.

She recognises the man that had been hunched on the bench outside the church.

She takes a good look at him. The poor boy's only mourner is around forty, smartly dressed in a dark pinstripe suit and crisp, pale blue shirt. Over his arm hangs a brown overcoat. His neat, dark hair is just starting to grey. He looks at her with an honest gaze but his slumped shoulders, those of a much older man, cause Eva to pull her shawl around her.

"Buon giorno, signore."

The man comes close to the edge of the coffin and peers at the body from head to toe. He seems to take in every detail, even in the gloom that is making its way with difficulty through the filthy windows. Then he steps away and looks around as though uncertain what to say.

"Who put this muck on his face?"

Eva hesitates a moment. "It is not muck. It is our tradition. I thought to make him... But you have no need to insult me, signore."

He rubs the back of his hand across his forehead and sits down on the front pew.

"Forgive me, signorina. I wasn't thinking." His head slumps forward. "May I stay here a while?"

She shows him her open palm. After a few seconds, his breathing slows.

"I hear it was a drowning," he says at last. *Annegamento.* He ends the word with a long O. "A death for those awash with anger."

She notices a staccato in his voice: he is not from this region. Maybe he could be Swiss. Or English. Sometimes she hears footsteps outside her window at night: travellers who have made their way across the Italian border only a few kilometres from Cannero by climbing the snowy crags of the Ticino Alps to avoid the police checks. She glances at his shoes: expensive chestnut leather with a flamboyant tongue lolling over the laces, no trace of mud or dust on his trousers. If he came that way, he must have brought a suitcase, she reasons. Or he could be an official of some sort. Even a diplomat. His clothes are certainly not those of a typical tourist.

"Why do you talk of anger at such a time. Why would this poor man be angry?"

"The quotation is from Dante, my child." She can make out the beginning of a smile on his face in the murky light. "The Inferno. Let us hope that his anger was not repressed or he will be doomed to drown for all eternity." His nervous laugh echoes around the rafters, reminding her of a scene from *Dr Jekyll and Mr Hyde*, a film she saw many times in Milan.

She stands up.

"I can see that you do not know this man or you would not behave like this. You could at least show him some respect. A stranger deserves it as much as a lover, after death."

At the word 'lover' he stands, too. "Did you know him?"

When she does not answer, he turns to look at the door, as if expecting an interruption. His hand strays inside his jacket pocket, then he changes his mind and withdraws it. For the first time, she feels afraid.

"Don't worry, signorina. I will not stay long and you can go back to your reverence." She stares at him. For a moment their eyes meet but Eva cannot read his expression. The crucifix still hovers menacingly over the coffin like an avenging angel. She can hear him whispering his private prayers.

"Signore, who are you? Why are you here?"

His face still twitches with genuine emotion.

"My name is Stephen," he says finally. "This man was my friend and colleague. We have come from England."

"You are no friend that I can see. Do you know how he died?"

"Well, he drowned…" A few seconds pass. "I can say no more than that." He grasps the bridge of his nose between his finger and thumb. Then, as though he has reached a decision, his hand drops and he steps toward Eva.

"His death is murder. I cannot say how or why." His voice tightens. "A terrible crime has been committed here and I can do nothing about it. A man in my position is worse than useless. A foreigner in a foreign land." Another few seconds, then his head twitches slightly to one side and he studies her face. "But you... a local girl. You could find out. Bring the perpetrators to light using your—"

"Me? Why me? I couldn't possibly..." Besides not being a local girl, she instantly rebels against his insane logic.

"This should never have happened, don't you see? If we do nothing, this... this crime... will go unpunished." There are tears in his eyes. "And it will be repeated. In these times, it is not only soldiers who kill. In fact..."

"I am only a... a girl. How can I—"

"I am not asking for revenge, signorina. Only truth. Just a simple truth. To bring this man's story into the light. Is that too much to ask of you?"

As he raises his voice, she feels the fear rising in her throat. She cannot help this hysterical man find any sort of truth. Even if she wanted to help him, it is too dangerous. Her terror must be clearly visible on her face because, abruptly, he turns and stumbles back towards the door.

Once he is gone, Eva quickly follows down the aisle to the door. She lifts and drops the thick wooden slab into its resting place so that he cannot return. She pushes her back on to its solidity.

The startling visit has left her gasping for air. Who was this stranger and what was his connection to the drowned man? And why was he talking about anger and eternity? Revenge and truth? Above all, why did he ask *her* to help? She feels a sense of danger start to suffocate her. He probably does not know that people who start asking questions of the authorities disappear, or end up dead.

Eva looks up at the murky dawn sky, grey-green through the tall windows. The padre will be awake soon, preparing for his early morning service. She does not have long. There must be something else, something to help her understand this mystery. Despite her natural reserve in the face of death, she starts to run her hands over the young man's clothes. She is not surprised to discover that all the pockets are empty. OVRA would have carried out their own search before handing the body over to the local police. Even Commissario Bianchi might have had a rummage before he went off to play cards. She runs her fingers along the seams of his jacket. Every seam and hem has been slit with a tiny knife, as have those of the trousers. She slips off his shoes and examines them. Nothing.

She hears a sound: somebody bumping into a table in the sacristy. Padre Giacomo must be dressing for early morning prayers. Time is running out. Where else to look? There must be a clue to the man's identity somewhere.

She runs her fingers along the seams again, this time with her eyes closed. Another bang in the sacristy. Swearing. Any minute now, the priest will walk through the narrow side door into the church.

Finally, she feels it. Just above his heart. A minuscule line of stitches that has been sewn inside one of the existing seams. Without thinking, she grabs her embroidery scissors from her bag and clips at the virtually invisible darn. Inside the false seam, a scrap of paper. Thicker than paper. A ticket. No, half a ticket: a stub. She has seen hundreds of similar scraps discarded like coloured confetti around the quayside. Before she can look at it more closely, she hears the creak of the sacristy door opening.

"Buon giorno, carissima mia!" The priest stumbles towards her, arms outstretched. There are dark circles under his eyes and his cassock has acquired new stains since the previous evening. "Did you pass a quiet night? No visitors?"

"As quiet as the grave," Eva replies. She stands up, takes her bag, and darts out of the priest's path towards the main door and freedom, slipping the ticket stub, with her scissors, into her pocket. She can hear the priest muttering something about making do with a quick and quiet burial, in the absence of mourners.

She steps out of the main door, blinking, into another stark, blue day, and heads up and out of the village towards the wooded areas that signify the beginning of the mountains.

After climbing for half an hour or more, she feels confident that she is alone. She takes out the ticket and peers at it. It has dried fully, but it has suffered the ravages of the hours underwater. There is no ink left on it and it is starting to shred.

But the dark blue colour has already told Eva everything she needs to know: The dead man had taken a trip to Luino, the town on the other side of the lake.

CHAPTER 2

A small, tufted black and white dog sniffs at the pile of shoes left by the fishermen at the end of the cobbled lane. He cocks his leg and darkens the straw of the soles, then lifts his head towards the lake, sniffing for the return of the shoes' owners. Every day, around this time, the local stray dogs wait for the men to come back to shore. Eva can often hear the men calling softly to each other with their plans for the haul. "Barely enough for a *ciuppin* soup!", they wail on a bad day, thinking of the watery broth that will be their supper. Or, when the nets are heavy, "I'll be sifting through this until dinnertime." Although she has not yet learned the dialect, Eva can tell their mood from the music of their voices. She recalls her mother's favourite saying: Men are never happy.

The sun is barely up as Eva approaches her home but her mother is already trilling away up in their first floor apartment. The sun does not reach this tiny street, more of an alley really, its tiny dwellings pressing together over it, as though intent on denying it of light altogether. Eva can see only a thin strip of sky, but she can already feel the growing heat hovering above the cool of the pebbles.

The little town of Cannero has become familiar to Eva, if not exactly held in any affection by her. She knows all its streets and their occupants, which people to avoid (for instance the grocer, who writes down details of each person's visit in a little book to show to the secret police) and which people are not worth bothering about (the priest from the big church, for obvious reasons). As for potential friends, she has seen some other girls her age who work at the brush factory on the lake, but the way they look at her as they return home, huddled tightly in twos and threes, has not encouraged her to approach them. Besides, what would she talk to them about? They are simply waiting for an eligible man to come and claim them.

She pushes open the gate and trudges up the tiny staircase that winds around the courtyard, barely a metre square, that her mother has filled with flowerpots. She ignores the scowl that Signora Catalino hurls her way through the dusty window of the downstairs apartment that looks on to the staircase, where she sits in permanent vigil, her face cloaked in black linen like a nun.

From her mother's high-pitched voice, Eva can tell everything she needs to know about Paola's mood and her present circumstances. Instantly, she knows that Paola has more than one guest, that this is the first time she has entertained them, and, thankfully, she is enjoying herself. She is speaking in a mixture of simple Italian and the few English phrases she picked up from the same English neighbour in Milan who taught Eva. Only her mother could make so much of so little language.

As Eva opens the door, there are shrieks of merriment. One of the guests has mimed playing a glissando on the violin at the same moment as the little dog outside in the street has howled mournfully. Eva hears Signora Catalino slamming her little window shut, although she is sure it was already shut when she went past. The living room is dark when Eva peers around the door. No light enters the window from the narrow street at this time of day.

In the gloom, she can make out the three women she passed last night on the steps up to the church. They are squeezed into the tiny living room, rocking to and fro in merriment on the fruit chests that her mother has covered with the embroidered cloths she brings out when visitors come, especially those with money. The women don't appear to recognise Eva. Still laughing, they beam their open mouths in her direction. "Oh, your beautiful daughter!" says the eldest, a woman of about forty-five, wearing a red velvet dress that is far too hot for the season and too tight for her plump bosom, which seems to be fighting for air. Her steely grey hair is piled up in an imitation of what looks like baked goods. She half smiles at Paola in a way that indicates they have been discussing the trials of motherhood. Eva gives a bow. Paola sighs before addressing Eva in Italian.

"Where have you been? I thought you were coming home before the burial?"

"It is over, Mother. There were no mourners, so the priest decided against any rituals. I went for a walk in the woods." Eva takes off her shawl and finding nowhere to drape it, squeezes it into her fists. "Who are these people? I wished to tell you what happened last night."

Paola ignores her and switches to English.

"Eva. My daughter." Her outstretched hand, palm up, appeals for sympathy from her bewildered guests.

"Pleased to meet you, my dear," says red velvet. The other lady, a few years younger, wears the customary over-starched beige linen preferred by the English. Her matching beige hair has fallen out of its clasp, and hangs like a clump of linguine around her perspiring neck. She reaches out to squeeze Eva's hand with her thin fingers, so pale they are almost blue, barely a few inches from where she is perched. Paola continues her battle with the English language.

"I present to you, Eleenora, Josephina and Ameeliora. I find them at the pasticceria, and I invite to look at our house. Are we not lucky?"

Eva nods and smiles at each of them, finally locking eyes with the youngest, a pale girl, about the same age as Eva, but whose milky hands and smooth brow show a different history, one in which toil and want have not played any part. Her eyes, shining with mischief, are an odd shade of yellow-green, set alight by the olive silk shift she is wearing. Eva imagines adding an embroidery of cream and flame, no, better, fuchsia. A spiralling waterfall of flowers down one side. She examines the pale face for improvements she could make. She adds a touch of apricot blush and (for the love of god, where are her eyebrows?) a darker arc above her eyes.

"Mama," says Amelia suddenly, her voice singing with a playful insistence, "Can I take Eva to show her around the palazzo?"

Before red velvet can answer, Paola starts up. "In which

villa do you stay? I have seen most of the beautiful houses here in Cannero. Such money and beauty. In Milan, we also have beauty, but the city is poor now." She trails off, then starts again. "But Eva is very tired, and, like this, she make poor company. She has to work sewing today before light fails. So, no. I don't think—"

"Mother!" Eva switches back to Italian. "I have been stuck in the church for the whole night. I need some air more than anything. I can work later."

Paola turns to red velvet with a sour smile. Her hand signals limply towards the door. "Mezz'ora," she says. Half an hour of freedom. The two girls stand. Eva curtsies again and they slip outside, down the steps past Signora Catalino's swiftly-turned profile and out on to the cobbled alley, where the small dog sits licking himself.

The girls smile at each other. Amelia's open mouth and rolling eyes suggest a victory that she rarely achieves.

"Back in England," Amelia announces, "I am confined in a prison." She has switched to Italian, which is assured, if a little old-fashioned. Before Eva can ask her if she means a real prison, Amelia hitches up her dress and runs down the narrow alley to the fishing boats, where she turns right without a look in their direction, and disappears under the arch to emerge on to the start of the sparkling esplanade on the western bank of the lake. The occupants of the hotels are starting to come out for their morning coffee in the sunshine. The Maitre D' of the Hotel Cannero is poised on the steps of his ground floor restaurant to greet people coming from the Luino ferry, hoping to entice them to sit outside, to eat messy sweet *bigne* while admiring the boats. Eva looks at the incoming ferry and shudders. It reminds her of a motorised coffin.

Amelia is running past the French, German, American tourists loudly discussing their travel or sightseeing plans. The English women's frilly dresses single them out from the rest, but their voices are only for each other's ears. Amelia runs like a child along the Viale delle Magnolie that looks over the lake. Eva watches the girl's head swirling as if she can hardly take in all this beauty: the mountains huddled round, eager to get a glimpse of the rippling expanse of water, the red and yellow houses smug in their proximity to the main attraction. Eva follows her steadily — she never runs when she is near water and does not want to have to explain why to this over-exuberant English girl. Wildness is something else she has learned not to trust. The image of the strange visitor from last night, his big words and his flamboyant manner, will not leave her.

She sees Amelia stop running and drop to her bottom like a toddler, her long legs flopping over the edge of the lakeside path, her shoulders heaving in dramatic sighs as she studies the horizon. After a minute, Eva catches up. She forces herself to sit alongside her new friend. She feels dizzy to be this close to the water. She turns away to study a seagull pulling at a discarded brioche.

"I can't stand it anymore!" Despite the euphoria she showed seconds earlier, Amelia wails, attracting glances from the languid coffee drinkers. "Two weeks in this place and not a thing has happened."

Eva smiles to herself. Try the prospect of a lifetime, she thinks. Is she supposed to feel sorry for this spoilt girl, who looks half her actual age? Who, thirty seconds ago, was running as though life had bestowed all its gifts on to her? For the first time since she arrived in Cannero, Eva feels like defending the sleepy commune.

But before she can reply, Amelia continues. "I made Mother book us on to the Orient Express. I had hoped that *something* would happen. Anything. You have read the book, I suppose?" When Eva does not reply, she laughs. "You haven't a clue what I am talking about, have you? Don't worry, I'll give you my copy when we get to the Palazzo." Eva mumbles a thank you, but Amelia carries on. "So there we were, on the Orient itself, and the train was full of piles and piles of elderly aunties, dabbing their dinner from their droopy lips." She gestures back towards the sleepy cafes. "All these frightful people. Just sitting there... ingesting. They are not even interesting enough to be *worth* murdering."

But at this word — *uccidere* — Eva looks up. Finally, she has a chance to speak.

"Here, our dramas are real," she says. "The lake, it looks kind, but it claims its victims without prejudice."

Amelia straightens up, her wide eyes locked on Eva's face. "So. Tell me. When? How?"

Eva notices the childish glee Amelia finds in tragedy. At that moment, she feels almost like Amelia's mother herself. My life has been hard, she reflects, but I would not swap it with this pampered infant. "Amelia. You should not be so excited. It is no joke when somebody dies. In Milan, the blackshirts tortured a shopkeeper to death just for—"

Amelia seems to have misunderstood. "I have seen these blackshirts, too. From the train. Those flames on their uniforms! They are so beautiful and masculine and — *so* — dangerous! Mother says the fascists get a bad press. I would like to see those outfits on the front pages more often."

A memory jolts Eva to her feet. Yellow and orange silk thread twisting and gathering around her calves, like fire, threatening to topple her over. She is five or six. Her mother shouting at her. *Come lui.* Like him.

"What is it?" Amelia is by her side. She grasps Eva's arm with childish force, unaware that she is hurting Eva. "Why are you breathing like that?"

"It is nothing," says Eva, pushing her off. "I am tired. Last night, there was a man who frightened me. Who talked of the same things that you do. A murder. It is not a joke. In this country our lives are never safe."

Amelia jumps away from Eva as though she has been scorched and sets off again along the esplanade. "Now you are telling me off!" she shouts. Eva glances up at the turrets that reach up the hill towards the Monte Carza. For a moment, she almost turns back, but the thought of her mother fawning over those powdered women stops her. She runs after the green silk form she can see bobbing through the pale figures gathering in front of the hotel menu boards.

As she draws close to Amelia, Eva's anger disappears. This child cannot be wholly blamed for her ignorance, after all. Who knows what they tell them in England about life in Italy, so many hundreds of miles away? As she draws level with the English girl, she sees a new darkness drawn across her pale brow.

"I am not a child," Amelia says.

"I know,' replies Eva. She touches Amelia's arm and the darkness lifts.

They turn the corner at the end of the esplanade to climb the hill past the school. The children are singing *Giovinezza*. The words of the fascist anthem, which she had to pretend to sing at the beginning of every school day, fill Eva with shame.

Ready to dare. Ready to dare.

Amelia is translating the words of the song with moving lips. This is not our future, the two young women agree with a shared glance. Both smile as they trudge up the hill. The dog barks its agreement with something.

The gates to the villa are painted in diagonal stripes of purple, green and white. Amelia pushes them open to reveal an immaculate lawn. Various playthings — a swing, a fountain, a croquet set — are dotted around the front garden like exhibits in a museum. Japonica, amaryllis and jasmine conceal the high walls. Eva smells a fish soup coming from the kitchen, the lobster on the turn. The dog follows them up the path to the front door. Nobody bothers to stop him.

"Wait until you see my room," says Amelia, as though Eva might be disappointed by what she is seeing already. She unlocks the heavy front door and pulls Eva through to a cool hall, adorned by white plaster columns under the windows, on the windows, above the windows. On each side of the staircase is a glass-fronted cabinet full of rifles and handguns.

"I have a special gift," Amelia is saying as she ascends the pink-carpeted staircase, "I can solve anything."

She turns left at the top to ascend another flight, "If you have a problem," she sings, "I am the best person to tell. I have never failed. It was me who got us the invite to this place, when Mother was sure we would have to go to Harrogate for the Spring."

"'Arrow Gate?" asks Eva.

"Death on a stick," replies Amelia. "Nothing but cake and pavement."

"Oh, I see," says Eva, not seeing.

Amelia turns to climb another staircase, this one narrower, steeper. "I have learned how to solve mysteries. It has taken me the last two years, but I owe it all to my acquaintance with Christie."

"Christie?"

Amelia stops in front of the last door at the top of the house. She pushes on its brass plate with her shoulder.

"You'll see!" The door finally gives way and light floods out, illuminating the girls. The dog jumps back.

Eva blinks as she enters a room that spans the full length of the house. It is painted pure white and, in the sunlight, is even brighter than the eager morning sunshine outside. It has little in the way of furniture. A small divan sports a crocheted blanket in squares of orange and green. At the other end, a chaise longue stretches under a golden silk shawl. One wall is entirely filled with a bookcase brimming over with books. But even these few items of furniture seem superfluous when the eye is so completely drawn to the beauty of the windows. To Eva, it seems that somebody has removed half of the roof and one of the walls and replaced them with towering glass panels that stretch to the floor facing the lake. The panels are made up of a diamond lattice of tiny coloured glass panes that send shards of brilliant light on to the pale wooden floor and the white wall opposite. Two open, clear glass doors beckon the girls to go out on a balcony lined with pots of Iceland poppies.

"I often sew for the people who live in these beautiful villas," says Eva, turning away at last from the view of the water, which has started to rotate and squirm before her eyes, "but I have never seen anything like this. Who lives here?"

"A friend of my mother's. A count or a duke. Thank God he is away this morning. When he is here, he is always trying to catch me on my own." She extends octopus hands and shivers.

Eva smiles. "You are lucky to have this all to yourself, then." She sinks into the chaise longue and sighs, a starlet at last.

Amelia has picked up the dog on her lap and is whispering in its ear.

Eva hesitates, then decides to take her chance. "Do you think there are English spies here? Could they be a threat to the Italians? There are so many tourists, I know. They come for all this…" She shakes a finger towards the window. "But could there be, among them, somebody who wishes us harm? Who may wish to harm Il Duce?" She mimes a quiet shooting, afraid even to say the word.

She knows her speech sounds naive. She could never ask such a question of her mother, or to her old friends in Milan. They would have sucked their thumbs and cried: "Boo hoo, why do people hate us? Is it because we have a bare-chested idiot of a dictator ruling over us?" But there is something about this girlish Englishwoman — her enthusiasm, a yet to be fully formed wisdom still manifesting as a search for truth. Eva feels emboldened.

And who else can she ask about these things? Her mother would tell her to hold her tongue.

"Why do you ask that?" offers Amelia.

"There was a man. Last night in the church. A stranger, dead." Amelia is staring at her, hooked. "He was English, but not a tourist. He had drowned in the lake."

"There are so many English here," says Amelia. "How do you know he was not a tourist?"

"The priest told my mother that the police had contacted all the hotels and private houses. Everyone is accounted for in Cannero. But it seems he came from Luino."

"Then surely he was visiting for the first time? A day tripper, perhaps. Maybe he slipped on the jetty and disappeared and nobody noticed for a day or two." Amelia is right, thinks Eva; she *is* good with mysteries.

"That is what I thought, too. I stayed with him all night. It was sad to think of him alone. But then somebody did arrive. What he said has made me think differently."

"Who was it? Why did he not come forward before?"

"I don't know. I didn't think to ask." Eva sighs. Amelia would have known the right questions. "He was English, too. He said… he said a crime had been committed, but one that will undoubtedly go unpunished. Those were his words. What could he mean? Could your Mr Christie help us?"

Eva watches as a smile breaks over Amelia's face, illuminating her mischievous eyes.

"*Mrs* Christie, you mean, my dear." Amelia walks over to the piles of books clustered around the chaise longue. She knocks one over with an elegant foot, then rustles among the resulting mess, finally selecting a book bearing the same black and orange colours of the blackshirt Arditi costumes. She hands it to Eva. "Here, see for yourself."

Eva sees her mistake. 'Christie' is a woman. Her first name is Agatha and she is a novelist. She is grateful to Amelia for not humiliating her, but there is a kernel of resentment inside her gratitude. She flicks through the pages.

"This looks very exciting, Amelia, but I told you before. We are not in England now. This is not a fairytale. Here, we are too used to death. In fact, we have to work hard to avoid it."

"I suppose." But Amelia has moved out on to the balcony. A tiny trilling song, like a goldfinch call, is coming from outside. Amelia peers over the edge of the railing, straining to see the boulevard at the edge of the lake. After a moment, Eva joins her. She squeezes Amelia's arm.

"I'm sorry," Eva says, "I know you are trying to help."

"You have to go," Amelia replies in a whisper.

"What is it?"

"It is my mother's friend." She points a tentative finger over the balcony. "I heard his whistling. He is coming back. If he sees you here, he will… you have to go now. Take the book"

Eva squeezes the book into the pocket sewn into the side of her dress. She follows Amelia, who is already running down the stairs. The dog nips their socks with his teeth as they jump on to the landings.

They whirl through the front door, down the path and out of the front gate. They are heading around the corner up towards the top of the town when they hear a shout.

"Amelia!"

"Is it him?" gasps Eva.

"Yes, but don't worry. He will not run after us. Not in public. I have to go back. I think he saw me. I am his guest so I have to…"

They turn another corner and sit down on a bench in a little glade of bougainvillea to get their breath back.

"When can I see you again?" asks Eva.

"Tomorrow, at ten. Here." Amelia gets up. As she walks back down the road towards the villa, she calls over her shoulder.

"Page 215. The last line."

Eva squeezes the book in her pocket and smiles. The dog follows Amelia back down the hill.

"My mother would call you a typical man," she sighs. "I don't blame you. I know which house I would choose to live in."

Then a thought strikes her. The book in her pocket is making her leg hot.

Books can get you into trouble. Eva has not seen a book in English since she left Milan. She looks up and down the road. A couple of old women at the bottom of the hill are dragging some branches from the forest to start their fire. First, she reads the title — Murder on the Orient Express — then she spreads the book flat on her lap so that no one will see the cover. She finds page 215, and reads the last line: "Let us all close our eyes and *think*…"

A simple line, she thinks. No hidden meanings or cryptic codes. At the same time, she is surprised at the wisdom in the line, its philosophy is not what she would expect from the exuberant, scatter-brained Amelia. She wonders whether all Englishwomen diminish themselves in this way. But there are more important matters to think about, and she does not have much time before her mother will wonder where she has got to.

So *think*.

She closes her eyes.

What does she know about the drowned man? He is English. And he has only one friend in this region who is bothered enough to come to his wake: the stranger. What were his words? *A terrible crime has been committed here but only you can investigate it.* Why me? The crime must be one that only an Italian could get to the bottom of. An Englishman asking questions would instantly attract OVRA's attention. One man has died already. Naturally the stranger could not draw attention to himself. But to ask a local girl is not only desperate, it is insane.

Eva thinks back over their conversation. Close our eyes and *think*. He did not tell her much about himself. But that, too, is natural, she reasons. How could he have known that he could trust her? All nationalities jump to conclusions about each other. This Englishman would assume that she is a fascist or, alternatively, a critic of the regime too frightened to speak out. But something about this man intrigues her. No, she cannot help him, she decides. Of course that would be ludicrous, too dangerous to contemplate. But there is no harm in discovering a little more about him. To protect herself, if nothing else.

Suddenly, she remembers the ticket stub that had been so painstakingly concealed in the drowned man's clothes.

That's it. Luino. She must go to Luino to find out more.

There is just one problem with that idea.
She has never been on the water in her life.

CHAPTER 3

When Eva arrives at the house, she sees the dog trotting past her down towards the harbour, where the fishermen are at last pulling in today's catch. He is hoping for a little crab to play with, thinks Eva. He won't get much more than that, she knows.

The house is quiet as she mounts the staircase that winds around the tiny courtyard. As she draws near to her front door at the top, it opens suddenly.

"Eva, *amore!*" cries Paola. Eva withdraws back into herself. She recognizes another mood of her mother's. This one is dangerous.

"Mother, half the neighbourhood will hear."

"Me no frego!" Eva shudders to hear the tired, but still sinister fascist shout on her mother's lips. *I don't give a damn.* "Hear this! I have sold a dozen napkins to the English women. And they would like three tablecloths in the same design. We have to start this afternoon. Do you know what holly looks like? No matter, I expect there is some growing on the other side of the road at the top of the town. I will send the boy to pick some so that you can copy it directly."

"Why the hurry?" Eva sinks into the makeshift chair that Amelia had occupied. She can still smell her perfume, a strangely adult mixture of cedar and rose, lingering on it. "Holly is for Christmas. We have many months to complete the work."

"My child," sighs Paola, trying to shift Eva off the chair by tipping it forwards, "These English women are organised. They saw my work and it set their minds working, working, working. They want to impress their friends at home with our craftsmanship, and they will have a story to tell, too, when they get back to England. They need their props! We can't wait until Christmas! We have no time to waste."

Eva knows better than to scoff at her mother's pride in her work. She stands up.

"Three tablecloths. Twelve napkins. How long can we feed ourselves on that? Three days?"

"Eva, you are not thinking, again. All our work is seen by countless others. Our business can grow from their admiration."

"Back in England, Mother? They have seamstresses there, I expect."

"Not with our skill. Anyway, what do you suggest, then, my little businesswoman?"

"We need more buyers here, on the lake. We need a marketplace that will sell our products to all the tourists, not just the ones you find in the cake shop."

"So now you are a capitalist! Don't let OVRA overhear your ambitions! They will be more than interested in the last capitalist left in Italy!" Eva's face darkens but

Paola continues. "So where do you propose to find your 'marketplace'? Are you going to set up a stall on the waterfront?"

"No," Eva smooths the front of her dress, feeling the book in her pocket propping its weight on her leg. "I am going to go to Luino."

She knows Paola has heard of the town across the water, has made out the long red roofs of the hotels on the other side of the lake, seen its tourists arrive daily at Cannero. Paola steps back. Her eyes are wide.

"But, you cannot... but, the water. How can you go to Luino?" Paola wrings her hands.

"I don't know. I will try not to think about the water. I will think about... other things." Eva shakes her head as though shedding an unnecessary skin. "The ferry leaves in half an hour. Put the samples together, Mama. I will get dressed."

Before Paola can object, Eva pulls back a curtain at one end of the living room to reveal her little divan that is pushed into a corner. From under the bed, she pulls out a crate containing her clothes: two work dresses of over-washed blue cotton, a pair of espadrilles and some undergarments. And her green shawl: a silken celadon square embroidered with a dragon of royal blue and flame, its eyes oozing yellow sparks. Underneath these, at the bottom of the box, she briefly brushes her fingers to her treasures: photographs of Hollywood starlets she has pulled out of the film magazines before they were banned from publication. Jean Harlow, Greta Garbo, Ginger Rogers, Katherine Hepburn and Bette Davis pout beautifully in silken monochrome, their features sculpted

46

from the purest marble. Eva shivers with the familiar pull of her ambitions. Also becoming more familiar is the sense that she is out of step with her peers, her family and her society. There were more dreamers in Milan, she scolds herself. But to escape the life that everyone expects of you takes more than just dreaming.

She straightens up and pulls the shawl over her head to cover her hair. It is a tiresome habit her mother insists on whenever they are out. She glances at the slither of mirror fastened above her bed. Her green eyes flash in the glow of the scarf.

Paola hands her a flax bag filled with single napkins, scarves and tiny handkerchiefs. Despite its small size, the bag is heavy with the silken strands woven through the strips of linen. Eva loves to watch the faces of her potential customers when she lays out these items that she and her mother work on throughout the night, the candlelight ruining their eyesight, allowing themselves only a few hours of sleep as reward for their labours. She smiles to see that Paola shares her pride, even when she does not approve of her destination. When Paola turns away, Eva quickly stuffs the English book down beneath the samples.

"The return ferry leaves Luino at two o'clock. Listen for the one thirty church bell to make sure you catch it. If you fail to come back, I will throw myself into the lake and sink to my eternal rest."

Eva kisses her mother on both cheeks. "I will not linger, Mother. And I will return with some orders. They may not make our fortune, but it will be a start."

The air outside is approaching its midday peak heat. But there is a breeze beginning to blow, causing Eva to

47

pull her scarf more tightly around her face. She ties it under her chin. The little dog is at the bottom of the alley, chewing on a piece of seaweed. It drops it when it sees her and greets her with a bark.

"Little man. *Piccolo uomo*." She tells him, "You are going to have to find something better than seaweed if you are going to survive." She grows silent as a couple of locals men, dressed in faded black, turn the corner. Mussolini is openly hostile towards the English attitude towards animals. Eva wonders whether Amelia has built a special house with a bed for her own pets, as she has heard they do. She resolves to ask her tomorrow.

Her thoughts are brought back to the present when she walks through the arch that leads to the esplanade and sees the little Luino ferry arriving at the jetty with its midday load. German and Swiss tourists disembark, eager to find their lunchtime restaurant. Waiting around are the sightseers who have had their fill of sleepy, beautiful Cannero and wish to return to the stronger pulse of Luino, that promises more of a bustling, industrial glamour.

Eva buys her return ticket from the kiosk and takes her place in the line. The deep blue movement of the water makes her shudder. The attendants look more like soldiers than leisure workers in their grey uniforms, their faces scowling. Occasionally, one of them lets out a scathing laugh and a comment in the dialect of the region. No doubt they are insulting somebody. The rest of the attendants chuckle with a barely concealed cruelty. Eva looks around for a likely target, but the group of tourists hardly merits even a comment. They look like all the others she has seen since she arrived in this town: bored and vaguely ill.

She turns away and views the mist surrounding Cannero island, a sad little rock a few hundred metres out from the shore. She has heard the local people tell stories of its decrepit castle housing renegades and escapees. Some more titbits for the tourists, she imagines.

Within seconds, she has been swept up in the queue and has hardly even thought of her terror as she walks down the gangplank on to the boat. The breeze has set up a swirl that gives the boat a small lurch. Eva, her eyes tight shut, grips the handrail and drags herself along the side of the boat until she bumps into a chair and table that have been screwed to the deck. She hears a voice, so her eyes must have been tight shut.

"You are frightened, child?" She tries to open her mouth but finds she cannot answer. The voice is that of an elderly woman.

A hand encloses hers and places it on the table but instead of the painted wood, Eva feels a fluffy softness. She opens her eyes. Placed on the table is a square of sheepskin, its fur uppermost. Eva, slightly appalled by its appearance, feels its warmth with her fingers. It is strangely reassuring.

"Do not be scared, my child. It is the best way to get over a seasickness. Place your cheek on the fur and feel the pulse of the most comforting of mothers on your skin. Its power is undiminished even though it is no longer living."

Eva thinks of trying to get up from the chair, away from this mad woman and her dead skins but there is another lurch and she imagines the water threatening to submerge the boat. There is no other way. Her head sinks towards the table and she feels the texture of the sheep's wool on her face, tickling her eyelids. The smell, rather than a feral stink, is warm and wholesome, like a nest she has made herself. As the minutes pass, she settles deeper and deeper in to the fur, her mind drifting towards an oblivion that has only comfort within it.

In what seems like no time, there is a shout from the guard to announce that they will be arriving in Luino in a few minutes. Eva dares not stir.

She opens her eyes when she hears the boat thump against the landing stage. She looks around for the old woman but she is alone at the table. All the other passengers are gathering around the lowering gangplank, eager to get to their long lunches. She cannot see her saviour among them. Without studying the piece of sheepskin too closely, she grabs it and puts it in her bag of samples. Then she follows the bustling crowd down the gangplank to the jetty, without looking at the water she has successfully crossed.

This is no time for celebration. She is here on a mission.

CHAPTER 4

Three men in black carabinieri uniforms, trimmed with red and silver, are lounging against the wall of the Luino ferry ticket office as Eva makes her way past. She pulls the shawl closer to her brow.

"Hey, *testa rossa*," one of them calls in her direction. She freezes at the mention of her red hair. They could be making flirtatious remarks or… they could be OVRA. She knows official uniforms are sometimes used to conceal the identity of Mussolini's secret enforcers. No matter who they are, if they find the English book, she will be locked up. Bowing her head, she hurries through the turnstile and round the corner to a small park on the lakefront where they can no longer see her.

She sits down on a bench facing the town. How could I be so thoughtless as to bring this book with me, she berates herself? Did she really think that reading it would be a pleasant way of passing the time during the crossing? Shaking her head briefly, she watches out of the corner of her eye for the guards, then turns her head towards the town of Luino. A wide road separates the lake from the large hotels that overlook it, giving Luino more of an urban feel than quiet Cannero, where the road runs across the back of the town, halfway up the mountain. And it is bigger, there are several restaurants already filling up on the other side of the road and Eva can spot three or four shopping streets stretching up and away from the lake. She decides to forget her covert investigations and get to work finding some buyers for her wares. Then she will go straight home to start work on the Christmas linen for the English ladies. Forget this silly talk of spies and crimes.

Out of the corner of her eye, she sees the guards are approaching, the embroidery of their jackets glinting in the sun. She gets up from the bench to cross the road, without waiting to see if they are coming in her direction. She rushes across the road in front of a passing motorcar, roaring North towards the Swiss border. Such machines are still a relative rarity around here. Back in Milan, she had got used to dodging out of their unpredictable paths.

"Signorina!" She hears a shout behind her. Without looking round, certain it is the three guards, she slips into the first building on this side of the road: a grand hotel. The lobby is filled with trunks and people milling about. She can get lost in here.

"Can I help you?"

A man in an old, battered dinner suit, complete with greying spats and faded patent leather shoes, seeks to restrict her movement with his hands outstretched. The hotel manager or the concierge, she decides. His eyes, a piercing blue, hold her as effectively as his hands.

"I am looking for… for an Englishman." She slips her

scarf from her red hair.

"We have many of those. Was there a particular one you had in mind?"

"Yes, of course. His name is Stephen. He is tall and has dark hair, about forty. He has a brown overcoat." She looks around at the men in brown; there must be at least ten. "Kindly-looking."

"Perhaps Mr Stephens is part of the film crew?"

Her eyes widen at the word 'film'. She has suppressed her thoughts of escaping into the film industry for so long, but the word still wields its magic.

"Yes, that's him." She smiles. "He is with the film crew. Is he here?" For once, she is glad that this hateful place, this cursed lake, has such a tiny, and nosy, population.

"I believe they are on location." He pauses before the foreign phrase. "I think that is how they put it."

"Yes. I thought so." She stands a little straighter. "He has asked me to work on the film shoot with him." The man raises his eyebrows.

"But he declined to give you his whereabouts?"

"Yes, I mean, no. I don't start until tomorrow. I just wanted to check that this was his hotel."

"Well, we cannot be sure, but if this is, in fact, the same man that we are speaking of, he will be leaving the hotel at the same time tomorrow as he has every day for the past week."

"And what time is that?"

"I am hardly at liberty to say, now, am I?"

Eva waits. A man can change his mind.

"What services do you offer the film crew, exactly?"

"I am a make-up artist, sir."

The words feel wonderful in her mouth.

"Really? That is surprising…"

"What do you mean by that? Not all young girls are satisfied by a faithless husband and an early brood, you know."

"I am sure of that, child. Especially not somebody like you." He begins to smile, too. "It is just that I hardly think that make-up would be necessary on this particular shoot."

"Why is that?"

"They are filming Mussolini."

§

Eva leaves the hotel lobby doing her best imitation of Bette Davis: with a wave of the hand and a resolute forward gaze. Even the doormen rush to assist her. Once she is back in the street, she becomes herself again. Glancing right and left to check for the guards, she pulls her scarf around her head and turns up the nearest side road. It turns out to be a quiet, climbing path lined with tiny, terraced buildings, many of which display wares for sale in their front windows. Jewellery, tableware, toys, hats, brushes, all types of local crafts are on offer to the occasional tourist who feels like dispensing with the midday meal and exploring. The local people are safely tucked away at their meal tables.

Remembering the originally agreed purpose of her visit, Eva turns towards one of the shops. It has green leather gloves and silk scarves the colour of quinces in the window. As she opens the heavy door a tinkling bell seems to stir awake the dark interior. Swirls of dust dance in the tiny shards of light coming through the thick wooden shutters at the back of the window display.

There is nobody behind the counter. Eva peers into a cabinet stuffed with silver goblets, candlesticks and clothes brushes. Another is filled with layers of fine cotton baby shifts in pure white and pale blue, tiny sailor hats and knitted boots with velvet ribbon bows. This is not like the shops in Milan, she thinks, which are filled with the latest in "Moderno" designs for the rich tourists. This place is from another age, aching with sadness amid a gentle hope. She feels both repelled and enthralled.

A sound comes from the room behind the counter, concealed by a thick dark curtain. Eva turns to see it being drawn aside. She expects an old man with a face of condemnation, but she is met by a young woman, her short hair the colour of a spring duckling.

"Ciao, bella." Her smile is as wide as her face. Another pair of piercing, blue eyes, thinks Eva. "How can I help you?"

"Ciao, signora." Eva pulls her bag close to her. "I am a seamstress."

"A nice job, if you don't value your eyesight!"

"I have no choice, signora. I work with my mother."

"Don't listen to me. My mother says my wit is crueller than a February snowfall. Sewing is a fine profession, and a necessary one. Are you looking for a buyer?"

"Yes, we embroider fine goods. Things like napkins and handkerchiefs."

"That is ideal. No time like the one we have here. Do you have some examples of your work?" She eyes Eva's bag.

"Oh, yes." Eva pulls a handful of samples from her bag. The woman rifles through with the tips of her delicate fingers, finally pulling out a tiny silk handkerchief in eau-de-nil, embroidered with a peacock in full display.

"But this is beautiful. It should be in a museum, not in this backwater."

At that moment, the bell above the door tinkles. The women turn to see the three guards from the ticket office shuffling into the shop.

Eva pushes her linens back into her bag. Women are not supposed to involve themselves in such bartering. At least, not visibly. The shopkeeper directs her confident smile at the newcomers.

"Buon giorno, signore."

One of the men is taller and older than the other two. His dark fringe is greased back from his forehead in a watery wave. The other two men are sniggering like the silly boys of her neighbourhood in Milan. Eva knows all too well how to make herself dull in front of them, to send them off to look for easier, or more rewarding female prey. But the older man has a different attitude. Rather than looking her up and down, he studies her face, looking for signs of nervousness. Or vulnerability.

The shopkeeper clips her heels together and gives an extravagant fascist salute. Eva quickly follows suit. As the guards exchange the slightest of smiles, the shopkeeper winks at Eva.

"Very impressive, signora," says the older guard, turning to Eva. He holds out his hand to her expectantly.

Eva searches in her bag for her identity card. She hands it to him.

"What are you doing in Luino, bellisima?" He studies the card with equal interest, copying her details into his notebook, and hands it back. "A boyfriend brings you here, eh?"

How she would love to tell him that she has no interest in either boys or the relationships they offer. But contradicting the wishes of Mussolini, even only in intentions, in such company is more than reckless. Instead, it is better to admit to the sin of commerce: "No, it is work that brings me."

"A working girl? But you are old enough to marry." A pause. "What is your profession?"

"I sew. I work for my mother." God forbid he thinks I am alone, she thinks.

"Let's see." He grabs her bag and pulls out some of the linen squares. He turns them over and studies their craftsmanship, swirls of bright blues melting into cream. He drops them to the floor. Eva quickly stoops to pick them up.

"What do you think, boys?" He leers at his comrades. One gives a slow nod of the head, without taking his eyes from Eva. The other murmurs, "Oh yes, Captain, it will do very nicely."

Eva gathers her samples together, snatching the remaining one from the older man. "I have to go now. My boat leaves at two o'clock."

The man looks at his watch. "Plenty of time, dear girl."

"No, she has not." The shopkeeper steps between Eva and the men. "I have asked her to deliver some items to my family before the boat leaves."

He smiles. "Still plenty of time." He turns to Eva. "We simply want to talk a bit of business with you. You know, I suppose, of the important visitors we have coming to Lago Maggiore?"

Eva thinks quickly. The film crew. "Yes," she stammers. "Il Duce is coming."

"You are ill-informed, dear child. He is already here, at the…. In the area. His guests are coming from England and France and will want to have the best of everything when they arrive."

Eva swallows. "What does that have to do with me?"

The man is leaning luxuriously against the counter. He gazes towards the shuttered window at the shafts of dusty light. "Mussolini loves beautiful things…" He turns back to Eva and smiles. His mouth is too moist. "So bring him your most intricate and beguiling work and it will be seen by the highest figures in Europe. Now that sounds nice, doesn't it?"

Eva looks from face to face. The shopkeeper's mouth hangs open.

"Or go back to Cannero and work yourself into your grave." Her chest tightens as the man pulls himself from the counter and stands upright.

"We will send a boat for you at nine a.m. sharp the day after tomorrow. Bring your best! Arrivederci, signore."

Before Eva has time to wonder how these men know where she lives, they file out of the shop. Their heels clip the wooden floor like gunfire.

"My name is Stella," the shopkeeper holds out her hand for Eva to shake. "But it looks like you won't need small customers like me, after all."

"Not at all," says Eva, holding her hand with both of hers. "I can give you my best price."

CHAPTER 5

Before she pushes open the door to the apartment, Eva has rehearsed her replies to the inevitable barrage of enquiries from her mother. Yes, she has been on a ferry twice and survived, albeit with her head buried in the skin of a dead sheep. She has found two new sets of buyers for their work, and one is Il Duce himself. She tries to anticipate how excited Paola will be at this last piece of news, but she has never experienced delivering any tidings as good as this. Her mother's clients back in Milan were once the best in the land, her reputation steadily growing. Here in Cannero, the buyers soon disappear back to their own countries, usually without even bothering to find out the name of the person who made their beautiful mementoes.

Eva can hear her mother moving about the little kitchenette that leads from the main room.

"In here!"

She squeezes in through the narrow arch, presses herself against the little cupboard they brought from Milan on a trolley, stuffed with threads, needles and paper patterns.

"I have so much to tell you!" The laughter in Eva's voice disappears when she sees that her mother does not look up from her chopping. The solemn smell of sage fills the room.

"Later, later, Scintilla…" says Paola, reaching for more herbs. "For now we have to get on." A jolt runs through her body. *Scintilla*. Little Spark. The only person to call Eva his 'Little Spark' was her father. Her mother carries on chopping, as though she has not felt the charge of his ghost disturbing the room.

"What is happening, Mama?" Eva tries to lay her hand on Paola's wrist, but Paolo slides away, without losing a beat in her culinary rhythm. "What are you cooking?"

"*Agnolotti del Plin*. And *Torta Barozzi*. No time to talk, amore. I need you to collect the holly from the clearing at the top of the town, so that I can finish this in peace. What time did the clock in the market square show when you passed by?"

"It was three o'clock. But why are you making such a dish? Do we have guests coming? Here?"

Paola puts down her knife and looks up at last. Her face is flushed but a smile spreads from her eyes. "Three o'clock? That gives us just enough time. By the time you get back they will be on their way. When they have gone, we can start on the napkins. Now, go! Go!"

But Paola has ignited this little spark. Eva stands her ground and manages to keep the emotion from her voice. All thoughts of Mussolini and his desire for napkins are put aside until her mother has calmed down. "Not until you tell me what is going on. Who is coming?" She has had enough surprises today.

Paola breathes out loudly, wipes her hands on a rag, and studies Eva. "You have grown up, my child. It is time for you to make something of yourself. I have met a woman today who has given hope to my heart for the first time in so many, many years."

Make something of herself? This can only mean one thing.

"How can this woman help me, Mama? I have everything I—"

"You think so, yes? So who is going to care for you when I am gone? Eh? How can I protect you when I am in my grave? Think of these things a little, child!"

Eva is silenced. The last time they had this conversation was in Milan. The blackshirts had taken the local grocer away, accusing him of withholding goods from his customers, keeping them for himself. He had never been seen again. The incident had changed the attitude of many of the locals, who subsequently sought to marry their daughters into the families of fascist officials, hoping that such a union was the best way to guarantee the family's safely. It had been the cause of many arguments between mothers and their daughters, Eva's friends. Eva had managed to stay unwed then. Another such fight now would not be so easy: she is twenty years old and in the eyes of society, quite ready for matrimony.

"Yes, you see? These are not trivial questions any more. Your dreams of make-up, films, glamour, whatever it is… they are childish. Ones that you have to give up eventually."

Eva puts her hand gently on her mother's arm. Paola looks up at her daughter with tears coming quickly to her eyes. "Who is this lady, Mama?" she asks, with hardly a trace of scream in her voice.

"She lives just outside Cannero, up in the hills looking over the lake. Her husband is no longer alive, but her son, her *son*," she looks askance at Eva, "is doing very well in the police."

Eva pauses. She longs to ask: which police force? Is it the one that directs the traffic and greets old ladies by name? Or the other one? She knows Paola is being deliberately vague, but she cannot face an argument. Instead, she says: "Then we have no time to waste, Mama. I will collect the holly for tonight's work and some extra candles so that we can see our work. Then, when I get back, I will help you make the Torta and lay the table."

Paola pulls her daughter towards her and Eva feels her familiar shape melt into her body. She breathes in the warmth and soft smell of her mother.

"Enough, Mama!" She pushes Paola away gently and reaches behind for her coat and bag. "Get to work!" As she pulls the door shut behind her, she hears Paola singing: "*Nell'alta notte brillano le stelle…!* The stars shine high in the night, but your eyes are more beautiful!"

§

The sun is still burning through the village as Eva walks up the hill to the wood. The road is steep and deserted. Not even the tourists walk this way in this heat, preferring to skirt the lake so that they can rest in a cafe when their clothes start weighing too much. The miserable shopkeeper's wife with silver grey hair as thick as angel spaghetti is behind the counter when she goes into the grocer's. When Eva asks for ten candles, she scowls as though Eva was depriving the rest of the community of light. She stuffs them in the bottom of her bag and races out of the door, relieved to be back in the hot air rather than the cloud of resentment that the local women so often breathe around her.

The same questions swirl around Eva's mind as she climbs the hill. Is her mother really serious about the marriage? How can she avoid such a sentence? And, if she can't, how can she survive it? All her worries about the drowned man and his English friend have been eclipsed by this new obstacle to her happiness. A husband.

As she approaches the woods, its inky scent starts to wield its calm magic.

She is rarely alone here. The villagers raid its stocks of mushrooms and berries whenever they can. And Eva often spots the familiar entwined shapes of courting couples in the dark corners at dusk.

Today, though, she sees no one. She seeks out her favourite paths that lead up to the clearing at the very top of the hill. Goldcrests explode from trees in a laughing tumble. Leaves purr their satisfaction to each other in the breeze. She pushes past the cork oak trees that shield her from the sun, intent on finding the holly.

Suddenly, she hears a noise. Somebody is walking through the trees, down from the brow of the hill. The footsteps are light, almost tiptoed. Eva draws herself behind an oak tree and waits. After a minute, she sees the form of the Englishman, huddled in his brown coat despite the heat, his hands deep in his pockets.

He is not filming today, then.

She is tempted to call out to him, but the same fear that took hold in the church immobilises her now. No, she cannot afford to get involved with him and his schemes, no matter what Amelia thinks.

Once Stephen is out of sight, she continues up the hill until she reaches a glade of holly. She takes the small knife out of her pocket and cuts the fresh ends of some of the choicest branches — there are no berries at this time of year, but no matter — and places them carefully in her bag. She is just about to turn on to the path, when Stephen comes into view, walking back up the hill towards her. She retreats into the holly cave and holds her breath like a fist. He stops within yards of her, cocks his head slightly, and then turns towards a storm-damaged oak tree on the other side of the path. Branches lay around its gaping trunk like a corpse's limbs. She watches as he pulls a small object, wrapped in a worn green handkerchief, from his pocket. He stuffs it down into the trunk of the tree, well out of sight. Seconds later, he is gone.

Eva waits a minute before she emerges blinking from the holly cave. There is no sign of Stephen. She goes over to the oak and reaches her hand into its soft entrails to pull out the package. She does not have to unwrap the handkerchief to know that this is a small handgun. She has seen a few of them before: the petty spoils of the war years, kept concealed but close to hand, just in case. She quickly replaces the gun in the tree trunk, before walking resolutely back down the path to the road. Her suspicions were right. This man *is* dangerous. She shudders.

She will have nothing more to do with him.

The sunlight on the road that crosses the top of the

village, where the buses pass on their way from Intra to Cannobio, is reaching its afternoon heat. Still breathing heavily, she surveys the entire village from her vantage point. Its small size, its eagerness to please and its natural protection from the rest of Italy seem dangerous in the light of this new knowledge.

An Englishman who hides a gun in the woods.

As she looks over to the right-hand edge of the village, towards the big church, she sees Stephen disappearing into its imposing doorway.

A terrible thought overwhelms her. Maybe Stephen is not the grieving friend that he appears to want to portray. In which case, Padre Giacomo could be in danger. Her legs are running down the track before she has given them the order to do so. She streaks back through the woodland, she cannot feel the branches scraping her legs, then out on to the road.

When she reaches the church, pinioned by its imposing tower, the great door is ajar. She runs into the vestry, pulls aside the velvet curtain and blinks while her eyes adapt to the light. She can see the shape of the priest kneeling in front of the altar. He turns round when he hears her and struggles to his feet.

"Can I help you, child?" He pulls his cassock down over the roundness of his stomach.

"Padre! Where is he?" When he doesn't answer, she says: "The man who came in a minute ago. The Englishman. Stephen. Or Mr Stephens."

"I am alone, my child. No one has come. Only you."

"But he was here, Padre. I saw him come in!"

"I have been here alone since mass finished at eleven

this morning." He lays a hand on her arm. "You are mistaken, child. Why do you wish to find this person?"

"I… he… dropped something." She feels in her pocket and brings out the only thing she has: the ticket she removed from the dead stranger's suit. She holds it out like a sacrifice. The priest takes it and examines it closely. She studies his face but his expression gives nothing away.

"It is nothing." But he places it in his own pocket instead of handing it back. "Now run along. Your mother is preparing a special dinner, I hear."

CHAPTER 6

Eva bursts through the front door of the flat into a pile of chairs stacked up against the wall.

"Where does all this furniture come from, Mama?" she calls through to the kitchenette.

"Signora Catalino, the angel. She keeps it for when her daughter visits with her family." Trust Mother to overlook all the glaring and tutting from the ground floor flat, and just see the goodness in their neighbour. "But, like all daughters, Maria neglects her mother. She has not visited since last summer. I pray she will come soon. La Signora's sight is almost completely gone."

"Not when she is spying on me," mumbles Eva, separating the chairs and placing them around the table. Her mother has already taken the sewing, cloths and threads off the table and piled them up on Eva's bed behind the curtain in the corner.

"Come and help me with the Torta Barozzi, Eva. My shoulder hurts."

Eva enters the kitchenette and shuffles around her

mother so that she can take over the whisk. As she gets to work on the egg whites, cradling the wooden bowl like a newborn, she thinks about Stephen. Where could he have hidden in the church so that Padre Giacomo did not see him at all? Or had Giacomo been deliberately concealing him? Why would he want to hide the truth from Eva? Are they both involved in some sort of plot? Could it have something to do with Mussolini's visit?

Before she can allow her mind to enter a cinematic realm, in which Eva, the heroine, uncovers the plot to kill Il Duce and saves his life in a dramatic, death-defying sequence involving her fabulous powers of deduction, her Mother comes back into the kitchen.

"I think that should be sufficient, Eva. The peaks will be like the Alpini if you carry on any longer."

"Oh! Mama, I'm sorry. Yes, that is enough."

Eva takes a handful of hazelnuts and tosses them in the mortar. She grinds them into a powdery grain, which she adds to the egg yolks, then adds a cup of thick black coffee, with another handful of the precious sugar that Paola has managed to procure from the grocery store. She has probably traded some of her best gossip for such a prize, thinks Eva. Finally, her favourite part, she thickens the potion with a melting chocolate and butter mixture. Before they came here, Eva would have poured a glug of rum into the pot, but a woman cannot buy alcohol in Cannero if she has no husband to please.

Eva takes the cake mould that Paola inherited from her mother, lines it with precious brown paper and spoons in the mixture, trying not to think about the evening ahead. A dinner with a potential suitor and mother-in-law would have been a serious occasion even back in Milan. Here, it will probably make front page news. Giacomo already knows all about it. The whole town will be talking of it tomorrow and she will be the victim of even more stares from the local girls, who will believe they should be chosen ahead of her, a mere 'newcomer'.

While Eva smooths the top of the cake, Paola keeps her hand on Eva's shoulder a little longer than usual.

"Thank you, my dearest child," Paola sighs and looks into Eva's eyes. "You are… You will be…" but her words, so long held back, will not come now.

"If you go and put that in the oven, Mama, I will finish preparing the table."

Paola pulls on her shawl and Eva hands her the cake mould to take down to the Hotel, where the chef, one of Paola's many admirers, will follow her stern instructions about the exact time to put the Torta in the oven, when to take it out. And he will still smile at her sweetly.

§

Between mother and daughter, they have finished all their preparations a good ten minutes before the guests are due to arrive. Eva, fearing that Paola will try and fit in a lecture on how she is expected to behave, busies herself behind the curtain, arranging her bag for the morning. Her gaze alights on 'Murder On The Orient Express'. She must return it as soon as possible to Amelia, she decides. It is far too dangerous to have an English book hidden either here or in her bag. It has already got her into enough trouble. She can read all the foreign books she likes without fear once she gets to Hollywood.

Suddenly, Paola pulls back the curtain and hands Eva a folded piece of paper. On the front is her name scrawled in green ink beneath the printed name of *Hotel Cannero*.

"This was pushed under the door while you were collecting the holly. I think it is in Russian."

"You have read the letter? Before I have even…? How could you?" But Paola has already disappeared back into the kitchen.

Swallowing her indignation in a movement grown worn with habit, Eva opens the creamy vellum and reads:

R OLQS ISVJ KA XKPG SICDRJOHLI. PIMRD MKHKGGKV. L

"Dear God," she whispers beneath her breath, "What is happening to me?"

Again, she thinks back over the day. She is certain she has never seen anybody Russian in the village. Could it be from the guards from Luino? The shopkeeper? The mysterious sheepskin lady on the ferry?

Her mother shouts across her thoughts. "Eva!" Then her voice softens into a welcome. "Our guests have arrived!" Eva pinches the skin between her thumb and fingers to remind herself to behave, to keep her mother's hopes alive, to avoid a midnight argument, or, worse, a week of silence, which will be the likely result if she does not appear to bend to Paola's wishes. She feels confident that she can put off a potential husband in due course, if that is what he turns out to be.

Eva emerges from behind her curtain to find a little crowd filling the room with their awkwardness. Three new figures hover around the dining table, trying not to press against the wall. A tiny patch of evening sunlight from the high window at the back of the room illuminates the tops of their heads.

Centre stage is a woman a little older than her mother. Every inch of her suggests Cannero, the weathered skin, the stoop, the fading black floor-length dress, the permanent wave slowly abandoning her hair. She clutches the arm of an upright young man in the grey-green uniform of the local police force and a shock of pale hair. On the woman's other side is an elderly man with a slowly healing wound on his balding head. He is already slumping into one of Catalina's chairs with a snort of relief.

"Eva! Come quickly and welcome Signora Bracco, and her family," says Paola, who flattens herself into the wall to allow Eva through to make her formal introductions.

Eva approaches Signora Bracco and waits for her dry kisses to scrape her cheek. Signora Bracco smells of lemons and cyprus, but her nails stick into Eva's hand with something like a warning. Eva turns to the elderly man and curtsies with her head bowed. Then she squeezes past Signora Bracco to reach the young man.

"My son," announces Signora Bracco, a solemn smile at last appearing on her weary face. "Welcome," Eva recites and reaches up to kiss him. He laughs when their noses brush lightly together. "Marco," he says, simply.

"Eva," her mother calls, "Go and get your chair from the staircase so we can all sit down." She goes and hauls the vegetable box back inside. The elderly man is obviously a surprise guest, brought along in order to prevent Eva and her mother eating the poor young man alive.

They all sit while Eva goes to the stove to collect the

Agnolotti del Plin. She checks the contents of the deep earthenware dish, although she knows already that her mother would never allow even one of the pinched parcels of flour and egg to have lost its treasured centre of pork, herbs and cheese.

She sets the pan on the table between the guests and Paola reaches in with her enormous wooden spoon she bought in Milan. Eva starts to pour water into their glasses but the elderly man, who still does not have a name, reaches deep into one of the pockets of his faded black coat to pull out a dusty bottle of *Amaro*. He knocks back all five glasses of water before refilling them with the terracotta-coloured liquid with fragments of herbs suspended in it like dirt. Throughout this ritual, Signora Bracco has clasped her son's forearm as if he might fall over the edge of a cliff.

Eva sits and joins in the toast.

"My dear guests," says Paola, lifting her glass with only the very tips of her fingers. "If only my husband were here to welcome you, and to a much less reduced household. Reduced… in many ways." Her gaze is with Eva, who drinks deeply. The taste of the Amaro reminds her of the wood above the village, the same scents permeate its murky brownness. She picks a stem from the tip of her tongue and hides it beneath her skirt.

"And where did your poor husband serve?" Signora Bracco voice scrapes into the room, making Eva's glass tingle against her fingers.

"Well, he was at stationed at Trentino, in charge of a unit of men, of course. But thankfully he never took his soldiers to Caporetto, as some of his compatriots did."

"The shame of our countrymen," murmur Signora

Bracco and her brother in unison. Eva remembers learning about the mutiny in her history lessons at school. The teacher had wept when describing how the soldiers, cold, tired and hungry, had let down Italy so terribly when they turned on their leaders, as though they alone were responsible for the deprivation that followed the war. Eva could not help but see it differently, even then. Surely they were desperate, she wanted to ask her teacher, who left the room soon after, sobbing and effectively putting an end to any discussion about why the Caporetto mutiny happened. Surely the Italian soldiers had no choice but to walk away from certain starvation and death? Why else would they carry out such a self-sabotaging act? But she quickly learned that seeing the point of view of the masses was not going to win her any awards in school, or at home.

"My husband died bravely, they said," says Paola, draining her glass of the last drops of the thickening liquid. "And I have my dear daughter to remind me of his noble nature." She beams at Eva in a way that is new and oddly sinister, as though she is building a character that will appeal to Signora Bracco, whom she sees as the buyer in the room.

"My son is also a credit to my husband's memory, signora… and I have a solemn duty to that memory." Signora Bracco turns towards Eva. "I hope your daughter is a true fascist, signora? She does not wear the Italian Youth uniform, I notice." Signora Bracco wrinkles her nose as though Eva's plain black dress is not decent, despite the fact that it stretches from her neck to well below her knees.

"Eva is a little older than she looks. She is twenty, signora."

"I see," although Paola's answer hardly seems to satisfy her. "And where is your family, signora? Back in Milan, I assume." Before Paola can reply, Signora Bracco fires another round. "I don't quite understand your motivation in coming here, I must admit. Surely… Eva, is it? Surely Eva could have served the fascist cause much better in Milan?"

Paola puts d own her glass and smiles with difficulty at Signora Bracco.

"My dear signora, my daughter and I were alone in Milan. My family was always a small one and when my parents died, I was the last one left. I felt that it would be safer for us here, where I could keep an eye on…"

"I hope that does not mean that 'only children' are a feature of your family?"

"No, of course not!" Paola gives a nervous laugh and reaches out her hand to cradle Eva's stomach. "No, we are most fertile! My father was one of ten, and I had four brothers, but they are all lost to me now. The Great War was a cruel one for families."

"Indeed… so you have nobody left at all?" Signora Bracco stares into the centre of the table as the air cools at this remark. It is Marco's turn to interject.

"Dear Mama, we lost family, too! Let us change the subject. We are coming together in simple celebration of a great future, as Il Duce has instructed."

Eva expects an argument from this formidable woman but her face melts into a beaming smile.

"Mio caro, my dear, thank you for the reminder," she coos, then turns to Paola, "It is my age, dearest madam. I can forget my manners, my humility, in an instant, especially when I am hungry."

"Mama!" shouts Marco.

"Ha! You see, I am doing it again! I am so sorry, signora."

"No, it is me who must apologise, for keeping my guests waiting!" She stands and starts to ladle the tiny parcels drenched in chopped sage and egg yolk into dishes. "And you must call me Paola, signora. In Milan, you know, we are more informal." When she sees Signora Bracco sitting up a little straighter at the mention of Milan, Paola adds, "But the warmth of the Milanese cannot be compared to that of the people of Maggiore."

"I agree, of course. And you must call me Carlotta."

Once Signora Bracco receives her dish, she puts it down quickly in front of her, drains her glass of *Amaro* and bends her head to get to work. Paola points to Eva and Marco. "You two must be dying to find out all about each other, eh?"

"Oh, Mama, really." But her mother waits in expectation.

"Alright, Mama." She sighs and the two young people exchange a grin. "So, Marco!" she begins. "I see you wear the uniform of the protectors of our regime. Is there really much work to be done in keeping such a gentle community in line? I mean, what kind of dissent can the tourists spread while they are tanning themselves on a pleasure boat?"

Although Signora Bracco does not lift her head from her work, Marco stiffens. "You have no idea of the severity of the threat to our beloved Italy, even here," he says. "I cannot talk of the things I see — we are told to shield the community from too much alarm — but I advise you to keep away from people you do not know personally, and even those you do not know *well*, signorina."

Eva feels her head start to spin. It was only a few hours ago that she was talking to the guards in Luino. Before that an Englishman with a gun. Her breath starts to quicken.

There is a noise from the corner of the table. Signora Bracco's brother breaks into life. "You can't tell me anything I don't already know!" he splutters. "Commissario told me yesterday at the card table. We have an English spy in our midst. A dead one, but a spy just the same." He recovers his composure, wipes his chin and turns back to his food.

"There, there, uncle. Remember that everything he tells you is just to put you off the scent." Marco turns to Eva. "Is anything wrong, signorina?" He stares at her, wide-eyed with accusation. "Have we touched on something... difficult?"

"Not at all. I was just thinking that here we are, the so-called youth of today, *la giovinezza*, and yet you call me signorina! Please call me Eva."

The room breaks into relieved chuckles. "And you may call me Marco."

The company return to their bowls of pasta while Signora Bracco's chaperone refills their glasses with *Amaro*. Paola, for once, is quiet.

"So, Signorina Eva," says Marco, "As a good fascist young woman, you are no doubt attending the workers' entertainment tomorrow evening — the *Dopolavoro* that our beloved Duce has arranged for our pleasure."

"I have seen the posters," she says. "I attended many such events in Milan. The generosity of Il Duce for his valuable workers is indeed endless."

"Our own display will be beyond anything you have

seen in Milan, signorina — I mean, Eva. We will be recreating the greatest battles of our history tomorrow night, using real aircraft and artillery. Better, eh? Admit it, Eva!"

While Eva searches for the appropriate response, Paola steps in. "Of course Eva would love to go to the entertainment. All young people would be grateful for such an insight into our great history. But my daughter has no chaperone for the evening, and I myself am unable to go with her, as my... ears are too sensitive to loud noises."

Eva looks at her mother, who does not meet her gaze. What on earth is Paola doing, arranging an outing without even asking for her consent? But then another thought comes to mind. What if Marco can help protect her from any association that she has inadvertently built up with the Englishman? Who knows what could happen if he should reappear? And Marco might be able to help her decide what to do about the gun in the woods.

"But I am happy to act as Eva's chaperone tomorrow night, signora," Marco is saying, "If Eva herself is happy to be accompanied, that is..."

Before Eva can reply, Paola cuts in, "Of course she is. Eva, could you go and collect the Torta from the hotel? It is sure to be done by now."

Eva gets up and squeezes herself past the guests to slip out of the front door. The little dog from the morning jumps up from its slumber at the foot of the staircase to run up the steps. It starts to nibble at her shoes.

"I will call you *Scimmia*, as you are a little monkey." She gathers the dog into her arms and buries her nose in its neck. "You better not have fleas!" She turns to see

Catalina staring through her window directly at her.

"Good evening, signora!" Catalina disappears quickly. "That has got rid of her," Eva whispers to Scimmia as she drops him lightly to the ground and they trot together out of the gate.

§

When Eva returns with the cake, the dog slips through the front door unnoticed, and, ignoring the guests, who are all laughing heartily at Marco's story, goes behind the curtain and jumps straight on to Eva's thin mattress, which is folded up in the corner.

"Marco was just telling us about the latest activities of Padre Giacomo," says Paola. "Did you know that he has had a door installed to take him from the vestry directly into the Taverna Nazionale next door? Now he can pop out for refreshments during the service without his congregation knowing!"

"Is that right, Mama? Whoever heard of such a thing!" Eva sets the Torta down in the centre of the table, which has been cleared of the dirty dishes. Somehow Paola has managed to wash them and reset them on the table.

"But is this a Torta Barozzi?" asks Signora Bracco. "I have not tasted this for many, many years. Where on earth did you get the sugar? We have been making do with dried raisins since last Autumn."

Now it is Paola's turn to falter. "I... I... it is the very last of the sugar that we brought with us from Milan." A clever move, thinks Eva. Demonstrating a superior relationship with the grocer would be the end of any alliance that Paola imagines could develop between their two families. "Saved for a most important occasion, our first dinner together, and the first meeting of these two lovely young people."

Amid general sighs of approval, and Eva's actual sighs, Paola cuts the cake and hands it round.

"Not bad," murmurs Signora Bracco, as she spoons the rich cream towards her mouth. Her lips strain toward the sweetness as it approaches. Eva looks away towards the elderly uncle, who has tears of happiness dripping on to the napkin on his lap as he sucks on his spoon.

"How long have you worked for the Garda, Marco?" Eva volunteers into the quiet.

"It has been my privilege and honour for over one year to serve our most illustrious leader in any way I—"

"Yes, of course, it must be a great privilege. And interesting work, too, here in particular. I mean there are so many different nationalities converging on this beautiful part of our country. How do you prepare for such a challenge? I mean, you can hardly be expected to learn Russian, for instance!"

"Russian?! Well, I have never encountered Russians, I must admit!" Polite chuckles are given through full mouths around the table. "We can hardly expect the Russian people to appreciate our beloved country. It is so far to come, for one thing, and their political climate is hardly—"

"Yes, of course," Eva smiles. "Silly of me." But it is too late.

"Why do you ask about Russians, Eva?" Marco is looking directly at her. "If you have seen anything suspicious, you know it is your duty to—"

"Oh, I know that!" She forces a gravity into her voice. "I take that duty most seriously! But what can I possibly see when I am spend all day and half the night sewing in this room?"

"Now, Eva, that is unkind," Paola cuts a second piece of torta, for the elders only. "Just this morning you came back from a whole night spent at the church. You cannot say I keep you prisoner here, now, can you?"

At this news, Marco straightens. "What were you doing at the church last night, Eva?"

But before she has time to answer, the elderly uncle intervenes.

"Ah, the wake for the drowned man. We all know about that. Just yesterday afternoon, we were discussing it at the card game up at the Becchetti farm. Nobody knows who he is, apparently. My guess is that he is a spy sent over to find out—"

"Uncle!" Marco's voice deepens in anger. "This type of idle gossip is forbidden us by Il Duce. He has decreed that our voices should be used only for profitable business and praising our beloved nation. You would not want me to have to arrest you for spreading rumours of this type, would you?"

Eva can hardly tell if this is a familial joke or not. Marco sounds serious enough. The uncle, however, slaps his arm inside the elbow, mumbles '*Roba dei Fascisti*' — Fascist crap — and goes back to devouring his Torta.

Now it is Paola's turn to intervene. "To get back to the *Dopolavoro* tomorrow night, then. Eva would love to go, Marco, but she has no means of getting to the airfield."

Marco's face breaks into a smile, relieved to be spared

81

the embarrassment of his uncle's shocking outburst. "It is simple, signora. I can pick up Eva tomorrow night and drive her to the airfield. I have the use of a military vehicle whenever I want. I am not on duty tomorrow night so I would be thrilled to accompany her."

"I would love to, Marco. It will be my first one here." She beams at the two older women, both staring at her. They are already imagining her in a wedding dress, she thinks. "I would be proud to."

§

Lago Maggiore, April 12th 1935

Dear Giovanna,

Have you ever wondered who would play the part of you in the film of your life? I would like to be played by Greta Garbo. Her haughty, disdainful face would suit the part well, don't you think? However, there is one problem. Throughout her life, when events have threatened to go in the wrong direction, she can raise one of her beautiful eyebrows and everyone would come round to her point of view. I, on the other hand, have neither the right beauty, nor the right manner, to make people change their mind so easily.

I suppose real life is never going to be like the movies. This evening, for instance, I tried the eyebrow-trick and it had no effect, when I needed things to change more than ever.

Where shall I start, my dear friend?

I know, with you.

How are things back in Milan? Are they still showing films from Hollywood, or have they been banned too. Maybe, if they have, I can find my exile to this place easier to bear. Maybe the Dal Verme is shuttered up, or only showing films featuring chest-baring youths exalting the future of Italy to the skies. Please let me know the worst when you write...

Here, until yesterday, there was very little to tell you. We sew, I smile. Every day passes in much the same fashion. But then, last night, an eccentric Englishman turned up at one of the wakes I am in charge of, talking of murders and revenge like a lunatic. I dismissed him as a typical madman, but I think it is more serious than that. I am now being followed by security guards. Yesterday morning they approached me and asked me to bring some examples of our sewing to show Mussolini. Mother was thrilled, of course, when I told her late last night. To think of Il Duce just seeing our goods, not to mention wiping his gross mouth on one of our napkins, made her weep with happiness. But I can't help but wonder how they knew that I was a seamstress before they stopped me. I suppose that around this tiny part of Italy, everybody knows everyone else's business.

Yesterday afternoon, I saw the Englishman again. He was hiding a gun in a tree trunk. I followed him to the church, but the priest said he had not seen him. You know the way my mind works. I am convinced that he is a spy, a dangerous one, or worse: an assassin! And the fact that Mussolini is visiting this area makes me think that Il Duce himself could be the target. Do you remember the story of the Irishwoman who shot Il Duce when we were younger?

In full daylight? Well, this man seems to have the perfect disguise. It appears that he is a film-maker. What if he tries to kill Mussolini when he comes here? You can see why I want nothing to do with him or his madness. It is far too perilous an association.

Anyway, I have other troubles to occupy me. You know how I feel about boys, marriage, the whole charade from beginning to bitter end? Well, it seems that being hidden away in a boring backwater with a population of two mongrel dogs and a few elderly women is not enough to keep such dangers at bay.

This evening, Mama invited her new friend for dinner, so that she could drag along her son, one of those panting, wide-eyed young men that we saw so many of in Milan. You know, the type that lines the streets in gangs to hide their embarrassment, eyeing the girls while pretending that they loathe the very idea of talking to one.

As this kind of young man goes, he doesn't look so bad. He looks like an Italian Gary Cooper but not so smooth. These men are either in love with themselves, and looking for somebody to add a new voice to their self-adoration. Or they are so insecure that no amount of girls hanging on their every word will ever be enough for them. I think he fell into the first camp. Certainly, his mother repeated his virtues at every opportunity, and has probably been doing so since he first appeared in her lap. How kind he is. How clever.

And how brutal.

It turns out that he is a member of our local *carabinieri*, stationed in Stresa, another tourist town a few kilometres from here. His mother never tired of telling us how, unlike

Cannero, Stresa has smart, fancy shops filled with fashions from Milan. She did not get her widow's weeds from any of those, that is for sure. She said that the hotels in Stresa dwarf the little 'pensiones' found here, and that real Hollywood stars stay in them regularly. Such as who? I asked her. But she could not name one.

The man-eating reputation of my mother and I must have travelled far and wide, because she brought along a chaperone, an octogenarian she said was her brother, who dribbled throughout dinner and only raised his head to shout 'Duce!' at inopportune moments. I wonder what good he could have done if I had decided to jump on his nephew?

Mama cooked her Agnolotti del Plin, which they ate with gusto and I made a Torta Barozzi, a heavenly hazelnut mousse that I served with the last of the strawberries we preserved from last summer. They brought a bottle of local wine that tasted worse than the water they scoop from the bottom of the boats.

But I am out of practice, Giovanna. Entertaining a young man is more complicated than it looks. My guard was down for one moment and I found myself agreeing to go with him to the Dopolavoro tomorrow night.

I have no time to worry about spies, assassins. I have to finish the embroidery work for some English tourists my mother has adopted, and then complete a few choice items to show Mussolini. What I will wear tomorrow night is hardly a problem — one of the advantages of only having one good dress!

My dear Giovanna, until I can come back to Milan to see you, keep yourself safe. And do not think too harshly of your cruel friend. I am slowly going mad here. And madness is often a case of being seen to say the wrong thing at the wrong time, which I do with ease.

With the tender thoughts of a sorrowful friend, I seal this letter.

Eva

§

She folds the two sheets of paper that she had pulled from the notebook she brought from Milan, and places them in the box under the bed. Ten other letters are already laid there neatly. Eva knows that to send them is suicide. The censors cannot take the truth and would condemn her for a traitor.

But she cannot lie to her dearest friend.

Even in a letter she will never send.

CHAPTER 7

It is already hot when Eva wakes.

She hears Paola sewing on the other side of the curtain, even though they had both been up well past midnight embroidering flecks of silver on to emerald holly leaves by candlelight.

Eva is glad to hear her mother humming her love song. She must have done a convincing job when she was nodding and mumbling her agreement as Paola listed Marco's qualities, 'quite incredible', and planned how the relationship could, and would, develop.

Slipping out from behind her curtain, Paola looks up at Eva with a face of pure joy.

"Eva, my dear one," she chirrups, laying down her needle and twisting her hands into a knot. "You have slept well and your dreams have been of children, I can tell." Eva is used to her mother's medieval dream-guessing. She gives a well-practised chuckle.

"I will make you coffee, Mama." She slips through to the kitchen and sets the kettle over the stove, which her mother has lit earlier. From its heat, Eva guesses her mother must have risen soon after dawn. She scoops the old coffee grounds into the saucepan, adds a pinch of chicory, then sets it to boil.

"Seven times, remember, Eva!"

Eva sighs and waits for the brownish liquid to push up its first bubbles, then she takes it off the stove to cool. Seven times! Although it is the only way to extract any flavour out of the damp, used grounds, it will take over an hour. She wanders back to the table and picks up one of the napkins that her mother has worked on half the night. Eva had stitched the outline of the holly leaf on to the white linen square after she had hemmed all four sides. But her mother has transformed a simple, spiky leaf shape into a living relief that you cannot help but want to smooth over with your thumb. The foliage shines like a river in sunlight, its contours moist and cool. Eva brings it close to her face to try and see how her mother has woven such delicate gold and silver threads into the myriad of greens but the stitches are so small that it is impossible to work out how the effect has been achieved.

"It is beautiful, Mama." She looks up from the napkin to see her mother staring at her, tears on her cheeks.

"It is you who is beautiful, my love."

"Oh, Mama. Don't talk such nonsense so early in the morning."

Paola wipes away her tears and takes up another napkin. The silver thread glistens under her thumb. Eva returns to the kitchen to put the coffee grounds back on to the stove.

She repeats the process another five times, going back

to the embroidery in between, where her mother puts her to work on the berries. Over an hour later, they are sipping hot, thin coffee the colour of lake water, a pile of completed napkins folded between them on the table.

"Will you take these to Signora Josephine's house and tell her that I can finish the tablecloths in two days?" Paola wraps the napkins in a sheer piece of cream muslin and fastens it with a thin sky-blue ribbon.

"How much do I need to charge them?"

"Take nothing from them today, child. I will collect the full payment when we deliver the cloths."

Eva shudders at the trust her mother shows in strangers. The fear triggers another memory. She has not yet had time to warn her mother about the English stranger. She has no time to waste. Who knows what he is capable of?

"Mama, I have something to tell you about the wake I was at the night before last."

"Yes, my child?" Her mother does not look up from her sewing but a slight tilt of her head tells Eva that her attention is hooked.

"Mama, a man arrived during the night to mourn the drowned man. An Englishman. I have seen him since and I think he may be dangerous."

"What makes you say that, Eva?" Her mother says her name with a special precision that Eva recognises.

"Oh, I don't know, Mama. He was not entirely — respectful — at the wake, although he said the dead man was his friend."

"And then—?" Paola puts her work down into her lap.

"Then, in Luino... I think he is staying there."

"But what makes you say that he is dangerous? Is he

not just another tourist?" Although she longs to tell her mother about the gun, something holds her back: her desire to protect her mother wrestling with her need to be protected.

"There is something about him, Mama. He has been hanging around the church and… the woods. He scares me."

"The church, you say?"

"Yes, yesterday afternoon. I saw him go into the church when I was collecting the holly."

Paola waits for a few seconds then speaks so softly that it sends fear through Eva's body.

"If you see this man again, you must run immediately and tell Commissario Bianchi. Promise me, Eva. It is important."

"It is probably nothing, Mama. I just wanted to warn you—"

"No!" Paola's volume rises. "You must promise me! As soon as you see him, you will tell me or Bianchi!"

"I will, Mama!" Eva grabs her mother's hands. "Don't worry, Mama. He cannot hurt me if I stay in the crowds. Please don't worry. Here, drink your coffee."

Paola takes the coffee cup and finally gives a small smile.

"Thank you." She takes a sip. "You are a good child. My only, precious child. I cannot lose you."

"You won't lose me, Mama." Eva stands and turns towards to the door. She cannot let Paola see how much she would like to be lost.

§

After her mother's warning, Eva treads through the cobbled streets with a new sense of caution. Since she moved here, Eva has not felt comfortable in Cannero, never felt like it was her home, but it has never seemed quite so dangerous as it does today. She hears the fishermen calling to each other. What tales could they tell, she wonders? How many bodies have they helped conceal beneath the water? She hurries away from the direction of the port and up towards the middle of the town. She passes the little church and inhales the incense that hangs in the heating air. She thinks again of Saint Roque's little dog and, almost at once, the little dog appears at the top of the road. Eva calls, "Scimmia!", her voice chiming softly against the thick, grey walls of the street and the dog pricks up his scruffy, wheaten ears and trots down along the cobbles towards her. As he reaches her feet, he sinks on to his back, his tail wagging furiously.

"Oh, Scimmia, you little flirt! So you, too, have to put on an act just to be loved."

His little body wraps itself around her tickling fingers on his stomach and the tail sends up clouds of dust from the cobbles.

"Come on, then!" He jumps to attention as soon as he senses Eva's departure and follows her. At the marketplace, she cuts across the square towards the bench where she arranged to meet Amelia. The book is still in her pocket, along with the letter. Perhaps Amelia knows some Russian and will be able to translate it.

As she approaches the little park, she sees Amelia sitting on the same bench where they sat together yesterday. She is wearing a different dress: today's is a soft mid-blue and white in a chessboard pattern. She is gazing out over the water with the raised chin of the tourist seeking meaning in prolonged leisure. Eva pats down the dusty hem of the tired black linen that she wears every day and trots over to sit by Amelia.

"Oh, Eva!" Amelia tries to conceal her excitement but her voice has too much breath in it. "I have seen so many soldiers here today. Two just walked down this road right past me. I think they had guns in their holsters. Why are they here? Is it always like this?"

Eva looks left and right but there is nobody to overhear her. She says, "No, Amelia," trying to keep a steadiness in her voice. She sits down next to her new friend, who is still twitching with the thrill of imagined suspense. "They have come to police the *Dopolavoro* this evening. It is a type of entertainment that Mussolini believes will keep the working people happy."

"Is that what those posters are about? But that is nice of Mussolini, isn't it? An evening out always cheers me up."

Eva cannot resist a chuckle. "Maybe some see it that way, yes." She squeezes Amelia's arm. "But most people call it 'fascist crap'." She thinks of Marco's uncle. He has seen too much of these underhand tactics, she thinks, but I am lucky: I already have my eyes open.

"So I expect you won't be going tonight, then?" Amelia pinches Eva's arm in return.

"Well, actually…!" Eva sighs and laughs again. "But so much has happened since I saw you yesterday! Let me tell you everything in order! Then you can tell me what it all means! Your problem-solving brain is just what I need to make sense of it all."

She moves closer to Amelia and tells her everything: about the guards following her in Luino and asking her to bring her embroidery to the summit meeting, and the Englishman hiding his gun in the woods, and finally about the dinner party, about Marco, his job and his family. Amelia interrupts only to check that she has understood the minute order of events. Eva, who has never had so much to tell in her life before, jumps forward in her narrative from time to time, only to hear Amelia cry, "Wait! When was this?"

Finally, Eva says, "And now I am here with you, which feels like the first time to myself I have had since I sat on your sofa yesterday in your beautiful room."

"I now have two questions for you, Eva." Amelia draws her hands on to her lap neatly and taps one with the other. "Firstly, are you sure the guards in Luino were following you from the boat?"

"That is where I first saw them, certainly. And I thought they noticed me, they called out to me. But I thought that might have been for another reason, because of their... masculinity."

"I think this is very important, Eva." Amelia doesn't see the rising horror in Eva's face. "If they suspect you of any involvement with the Englishman, then asking you to come to meet Mussolini could be a trap to get you on your own in a place where there will be many soldiers."

"I remember now. They said they would collect me from Cannero tomorrow morning. How could they know that if they had not been following me?"

Amelia stays silent but Eva's mind works noisily. Could

these men really have been seeking out her work to show Mussolini? Even with her mother's reputation this seems unlikely. "Look," she says, "I have some of the napkins your mother ordered. The holly is beautiful." As Eva pulls the pieces of linen from her bag, a piece of paper falls on to the ground.

"Oh God! How could I forget this?" cries Eva, stooping to pick it up. "You are right. What is the use in hoping for the best? This came for me last night. I think it is in Russian. What is going on, Amelia?"

Eva is shocked to see Amelia smile as she takes the piece of paper and unfolds it. "Oh, you are the sweetest thing, Eva!" Eva's look of alarm turns to incomprehension, despite the warmth of Amelia's voice. "I sent you this! And it is not Russian — it is in code!" Amelia pronounces the word in Italian — *codice* — with a smile.

"What?" For the second time since they met, Eva feels a world away from her new friend. "But this is no time for games! There are guns involved. Somebody could get hurt!"

Amelia takes Eva's hands and strokes them. "I know you are cross and I am sorry for frightening you. But this could save your life, not hurt it."

Eva looks at the crowd of letters on the page. "I don't see how."

"You told me that saying or having the wrong thing can incriminate you," continues Amelia, "so knowing code at such a time is not a game. It allows you to conduct your life without fear."

Eva remains silent. Besides everything else, she does not like to be made to look like a fool.

"You remember yesterday when we parted, I gave you

a line from the book to read?"

"Yes, but I thought that was just a good piece of advice."

"Well, it is always good advice to be told to close your eyes and think! But I meant the line to be more than just that. It acts as the key to the writing on the paper. Look!"

Amelia takes a pen and pad from her pocket and Eva watches as she writes down the letters from the Agatha Christie text without any spaces:

LETUSALLCLOSEOUREYESANDTHINK

Then she starts to write the alphabet underneath. "So you see I write an A underneath the L, and then a B underneath E. You know the English alphabet, yes?" Eva nods as Amelia continues to fill in the letters on the second line:

LETUSA
ABCDEF

Eva watches, fascinated. "Now, when we get to this next L," says Amelia, "we can't allow it to represent G as well as A, so we leave it out. And the same goes for this next L. So when we get to the C, we allocate the G to it. Then carry on until we have run out of letters from the original quotation." She scribbles to the end of the line and shows Eva the result:

LETUSALLCLOSEOUREYESANDTHINK
ABCDEFxxGxHxxxxIxJxxxKLxMNxO

"But that is only just over half of the letters accounted for? What happens if your message includes the letters from the rest of the alphabet?" Eva is tempted to revert to her original view of the English girl — as a spoilt girl to whom life is a long joke — but speaks with a mother's indulgent tone for the time being.

"Ahh! There are several answers to that question!" Eva sighs, her patience is running thin. "But the easiest solution is to add all the letters that don't appear in the quote in alphabetical order to the bottom line."

Amelia quickly inserts the remainder of the alphabet at the end of the line:

LETUSALLCLOSEOUREYESANDTHINK
ABCDEFxxGxHxxxJxxKLxMNxOPQRSTUVWXYZ

"Now we allocate all the letters that were not used in the original quotation. That is a bit tricky to work out, but not impossible." Amelia bends her head low over the paper on her knees and hums an ABC song to herself several times. Eva's head tilts indulgently.

"When you have finished, you simply rearrange the code into alphabetical order."

She has played this game before, thinks Eva, who watches her scribble her long lines, occasionally chewing the end of her pencil as she orders the letters. Then she presents Eva with the final code, smoothing it across her knees with a small slap. Eva studies the two lines:

LETUSACORYNDHIKBFGJMPQVWXZ
ABCDEFGHIJKLMNOPQRSTUVWXYZ

After a few seconds, she looks up at Amelia. "Right! Let's see what this 'Russian' message was that you sent me!" She grabs the pen from her friend and, still smiling, starts to add the letters beneath the strange words from last night's letter. Finally, she reads, "'I have news of your Englishman. Until tomorrow. A.'" She screws up the paper. "Do I need to burn this now?"

"Definitely!" Amelia laughs but her face quickly recovers its seriousness. "But don't you want to hear my news? About Stephen?"

"Of course I do, but I am tempted to wash my hands altogether of this little saga. Surely, it is possible that the whole series of events is just a coincidence. And if my mother finds out that I have been poking around in such a dangerous world, she will kill me."

"Look, Eva," Amelia takes her hands again. "I think you are too mixed up in this to back down now. In fact, I think you are going to be interested when you hear what I have to say."

Eva sighs. "Then tell me."

"Yesterday afternoon, we were at tea when the Count came in — you know the man whose house I am staying in — and he started moaning to my mother and me about a meddling Englishman. I kept quiet so that I would not give away that I thought I knew, or at least suspected, who he was talking about. He said that he is assisting the British Prime Minister at the Borromeo Palace tomorrow and that he did not want this 'Stephen' anywhere near the place. He said that he should not be allowed in if he tries to get in with his press pass."

Eva jumps up. "I knew it!" She walks up and down a

few paces. "Why else would he hide a gun in the woods if he did not want to—"

"Wait, Eva! We don't know anything for sure." She pulls her friend back down to the bench. "This Count... I have told you. He is trying to impress me. And he gets, well, irritated with people he doesn't like. And types of people he disapproves of. I am not sure we can trust anything he says."

"You must find out more from him. Why is he going to Borromeo? And why he hates Stephen."

"Yes, I will. He will be at luncheon today and wants to take a walk with me afterwards. I have always refused before but today I will go with him."

Her head is so full of disturbing thoughts as she leaves the park that she doesn't notice that Scimmia has trotted after Amelia.

CHAPTER 8

Eva stretches her arms above her head and feels the creak of her spine as each bone falls into place. She has spent the eight hours since she left Amelia, bending over her sewing, churning out bright holly and crisp mistletoe.

But if her mother does not complain about the pain, how can she?

Behind her curtain, she takes off her plain shift and replaces it with her Sunday best, a black dress, heavy and worn, to which she adds an ornate collar of white lace.

"You look beautiful." Her mother has crept into the room and squeezes her waist.

"Oh, Mother." Eva feels the warmth of Paola's hard-won approval.

"And I feel… oh, I know I am a crazy old woman, but I feel you will marry this Marco! Imagine, a fascist! I will be so proud."

Eva can hardly manage a shrug at this prospect, but she knows her mother will expect more than that.

"Marrying a soldier would make us safer, I suppose.

He is hardly likely to arrest one of his own family, after all."

Paola takes a step back.

"But why should we be under suspicion, when we have done nothing wrong?"

Eva pulls her brush roughly through her hair. "Don't worry, mother. I keep to myself. There is no suspicion aimed at us."

A knock at the front door, at the same moment the clock in the square begins to chime, brings a broad smile to Paola's face, making her look, for a moment, like a young girl.

"And he is punctual, too!"

Eva opens the door to find Marco brushing the dust from the shiny epaulettes of his uniform. He clips his heels together and gives a playful salute.

"Good evening, Signorina." He has forgotten already how she likes to be addressed.

"Hello, Marco."

Eva turns quickly away, as though she has lost something.

§

"What are you doing?"

Eva looks up. She has bent over to tie the lace of her shoe, which has somehow come undone during the bumpy ride. Marco turns off the engine of the army vehicle he has borrowed. Eva is so stiff from sewing all day that bending over is proving difficult.

"My shoe—" she mutters helplessly.

"Allow me." With one move, he slides over to her side of the vehicle, jumps out and bends over her foot. His knees are deep in dust and some people walking to the display start to stare at the sight of a man in uniform at the feet of a young woman.

Eva looks at the people who have walked miles from the surrounding towns to witness the show. Somehow, the tourists have known to stay away. The dust from their tramping lifts to form a gentle cloud around the form of Marco at her feet.

He rises and they take their place in the parade of people walking up the hill. Eva spots some girls from the Cannero Brush factory bounding by. They clutch each other as they laugh and call out to the young men in uniform who line the route. Eva almost envies them for their easy friendships, their acceptance of their roles as future wives. Above all, for their facility in making the most of what is on offer. The young men smile back, their eyes twinkling.

She takes Marco's arm. If she is to find out anything tonight, she will have to gain more than just his trust.

"Why are we going up so high, Marco? In Milan, the Dopolavori are always in theatres or music halls."

"Did you not read the poster, little Eva?" She does not tell him that she would rather have spat at it. "This Dopolavoro is a special one." Eva mimes a fascination she does not feel. "Yes, we are honoured this evening to be entertained by the militia's brand-new airplanes."

Eva lets out a small wail of wonderment.

"Yes, the Caproni Ca. 135 will be on show to the public for the very first time. It will participate in a display with the existing Savoia-Marchetti squadrons. You will see both the Sparrowhawk and the Pipistrelle in action this evening, you lucky girl."

Eva can hardly resist faking a yawn. They have reached the top of the hill to find clumps of people standing around. They look across to the hill opposite where the aircraft are lined up, facing into the valley between them and the spectators. Although the daylight is not yet starting to fade, there are torches ready to be lit to guide the aircraft back to the airstrip that has been hastily drawn with chalk along the top of the hill.

Marco guides her through the crowd to a cart selling fresh lemon cordial in tin cups. As they sip their under-sweetened drinks, Eva begins her undercover work:

"There is a good turnout tonight. I am hardly surprised since it is such an interesting and awe-inspiring spectacle on offer."

"Yes, our people deserve such a treat. We work so hard and, unfortunately, the rewards are still slow in arriving."

"But are the authorities not wary of parading our airpower in front of such a general audience? Is there not a risk of giving away our secrets to the wrong person?"

Marco, who has been scrutinising the lighting of the flares, turns to look at her.

"But this is the second time you have brought this up, Eva. Are you obsessed with the subject of espionage, or is there something you haven't told me?"

Once again, Eva wishes that Amelia could take her part in this play-acting. I have not read enough novels to know how to do this properly, she berates herself.

"No, I... I..."

"I am just teasing you, Eva!" Marco nudges her until she joins in with his laughter. "Italy only has allies! It is natural to want to see us regain our former glory on the international stage, is it not?"

"Of course it is, Marco. We… we deserve it." She bites her lip. It feels like the first, serious lie she has told as an adult. "Nobody wants to see others hurt."

"You are right, Eva!" She sees Marco warming to the theme. "Nobody wants that. And I… I only want you to have good things. Like this evening!"

"Then why were you so different last night, when your uncle was talking about the drowned man. You said you would arrest him."

Marco points his brow beyond the horizon. "Ah, my uncle represents the old, tired generation too well. He looks everywhere for subterfuge, for threats, and trusts no one, not even his friends. Our new generation believes in better. We want to work together to bring the future about."

Eva has heard this argument before, a common one among the young boys in Milan. She is not sure that dismissing the older generation is either fair or wise. When she thinks of her mother's inexplicable actions, she can understand the inclination to do so. But she does not want to get on the wrong side of Marco. She has to think, fast.

"But why are there no tourists here, Marco?" She squeezes his hand to divert any suspicions he might have about her motives. "Surely, we have nothing to hide from other nationalities, if what you say is true?"

"They put the wrong date on the posters," sniggers Marco. "On purpose, of course. The Dopolavoro is not a secret, but it is a reward for local working people, not a free entertainment for the rich playboys of the world."

Eva looks around at the thin faces of the assembled people. For the most part, they look drawn and gloomy. She is sure they would prefer to have more food on their tables than an airshow.

"Besides," continues Marco, "we most certainly have the support of other countries." He hesitates a moment and looks behind him. "I should probably say nothing about this, but, since you are curious about how we are viewed on the international stage, it seems relevant to mention that Mussolini himself has invited two of the West's most powerful leaders to this very lake tomorrow!"

Eva's wide stare conceals an avalanche of thoughts. If she reveals that she knows about Mussolini's visit, she will have to tell him that she was followed in Luino. If he suspects her of coming to the attention of Il Duce's security guards, he will tell her nothing about the local police's investigations of the drowned man and his association with the Englishman. If she should bump into Marco tomorrow, then so be it. Her safety depends on finding out what is going on.

"Here?" she gasps. "To swim? Or to sail?"

"Oh, Eva! You are such a sweet thing!" Marco hugs her tight, his breath warming her hair. "Of course not! He is signing a treaty with Britain and France. The formalities will take place at the Borromeo Palace."

Eva keeps the delight on her face. "But that is wonderful! Britain and France! Will you be going?"

"But, of course. The National guards have asked for the assistance of local militia in identifying any undesirables in the area."

A small wave of applause gathers strength as around thirty airmen appear across the hill. One or two of them, dressed in crisp navy uniform, give a wave to the crowd, but most are looking at the horizon, where a cluster of low grey clouds is looming.

"We are not expecting any trouble, of course," continues Marco. "There is nobody that can do us any harm. In fact, we only have the one unsolved case. Oh, I remember now, you know about that one: the drowned man."

Eva waits a few seconds. "Oh yes, the drowned man. I had almost forgotten about him. So nobody knows anything about him… quite a local mystery."

"Well, most people would have found nothing." His chin stretches with pride. "His wallet and his identity card had been taken, of course. But you can normally find something, if you don't give up too easily."

Eva waits, pretending to be mesmerised by the pilots lifting up the metal noses of the two Caproni aircraft in order to climb into their jaws.

"It has become almost commonplace to sew possessions into the seams of clothing," he says. "I can't think why people still do it."

Eva remembers the shattered seams in the drowned man's suit. So it was Marco who had cut into them.

"But you found nothing that helped you identify him?" Her level tone betrays none of her excitement.

"No, not really. Just a letter addressed to somebody called Matteo. The usual stuff. You know. 'If you are reading this, it is because I am dead, etc.'"

This does not sound so usual to Eva. So the man suspected that he was going to be killed? Surely, that changes everything? And who is Matteo? Surely, he deserves to know that his friend has died. Could finding this friend be the important task that Stephen wanted her to carry out? But how can she find him?

Wary of arousing Marco's suspicions, she watches the aircraft, whose engines fire into life on the hill opposite.

"Will you be trying to locate this Matteo? Perhaps he can shed some light on who the dead man is?"

"We hardly have the time." Marco sighs. "But I suppose I can do some routine enquiries once this visit is over." He turns to look Eva. "If that would please you?"

She laughs and holds her hand up above her eyes to squint at the planes, now ambling into life and heading for the prow of the hill for take-off. "Oh, not on my account! As you say, he is probably just a tourist who fell in the lake."

"Indeed." He looks at her a little too long for her liking. "No doubt, the Embassy will be in touch once they realise one of their countrymen is missing." He sighs again and turns to look at the take-off, which is drawing some admiring noises from the crowd.

"And in the meantime Il Duce will be coming here tomorrow! What an honour!" Eva almost has to shout over the noises of the engines, but nobody seems to take any notice. "But, Marco, how do you know that there is no one else who poses a danger to Mussolini?"

"Because we have locked up all the suspected dissidents by now." Marco's face shows that he is proud of this heavy-handed achievement of his unit. "Along with anybody else with criminal tendencies."

He puts his arm around Eva and she allows him to pull

her closer to his side. "In fact," he says, "Lake Maggiore is probably the safest place to be on the whole planet at the moment."

The crowd watches the Caproni aircraft take off, followed by a formation of smaller ones. But dark clouds have gathered above them and once the aircraft are a few feet off the ground they disappear from view altogether leaving only a faint rumble.

So much for the airshow, thinks Eva.

As the crowd turn to walk back down the hill, their moans are punctuated by more than one cry of 'Roba dei Fascisti'.

Fascist crap.

Eva thinks of the last person who uttered those words and wonders whether Marco has locked up his own uncle for the visit of Mussolini.

CHAPTER 9

There is still no sign of Scimmia as Eva emerges into another bright blue day.

She is dressed in her best Sunday dress and her mother has stayed up all night sewing her a brooch resembling the fasces, a bundle of sticks wound with a golden thread. Eva shudders as her fingers brush the ornament.

As she walks down the cobbled road, clutching the hessian bag containing the very best of their samples, something snags at Eva's conscience, on top of the sense of foreboding at meeting Mussolini. Her worries about Stephen have largely been allayed by Marco. What harm can he do? He was probably hiding the gun as a simple precaution against the over-zealous carabinieri around here. And his concern for his friend at the wake is natural, given that he has lost somebody close to him. Matteo, the man mentioned in the letter Marco found concealed in the drowned man's suit, must be a good friend, who deserves to be informed. But a threat to the state? Eva does not know what to think.

Amelia had left another letter for Eva last night at the apartment. A glance told Eva that it was in the same 'Russian' script, but she did not have time to translate and read it. Her mother had enlisted Eva's help in finishing the samples for Mussolini, before she had collapsed on to her bed fully clothed.

It is Eva's own failure as a friend that preys on her mind. Amelia had been spending time with her host, who did not seem like the most chivalrous of men.

Eva shrugs off her guilt and thinks instead about how she will greet Il Duce. She has never had to make a fascist salute and she earnestly desires to keep it that way. But if she is face to face with him, surely she cannot avoid it? Paola's words ring in her ears. "The proudest day of my life." If she refuses to salute and word gets back to her mother... well, it is unthinkable. She could even be thrown into prison. She could never do that to Paola, not least because the consequences would be so extreme. The problem threatens to overwhelm her, so, with infinite sense, she decides to do what is necessary.

She only has to wait a minute or two at the dock before a motorboat with a military flag pulls up, its engine roaring like one of the aeroplanes from the night before. The unbearable noise is all part of the show of power, thinks Eva, as all the coffee drinkers and amblers turn to look. Eva recognises the older soldier from Luino on board, but his two assistants have been replaced with a different pair, equally as young and gormless as the last.

"Eh!" the older man shouts, as they approach the landing stage, and gestures towards Eva, as though he wants her to jump in the boat while it is still moving. Eva spots her mother beaming among a group of local onlookers, no doubt gathered by her mother to demonstrate to the town their newfound nobility. Eva waves and turns back to the lake, where the boat is now circling in an angry sweep of spray. Eventually, the boat comes to a standstill.

"Not brought your sea legs?" He holds out his hand to guide Eva on to the makeshift gangplank that the boys have pulled from beneath the deck. She shuts her eyes as her body adjusts to the movement of the water. "And not from Maggiore, either."

"I'll get used to it," she groans. She longs for her sheepskin, that she left under her bed — it is not a day to be showing weakness of any kind. She tries to imagine its smell and its softness. She breathes in deeply and turns to look back again to the little crowd, fast disappearing on the harbour. She does not know why it feels like the last time she will see her mother in this way, as though she is leaving behind her girlhood, as well as her home for the day.

The men say little on the journey. Through her almost shut eyes, she can make out that one of the younger ones is doing something with his tongue while he steers the boat, which the other one finds hilarious, and his face reddens with unpermitted laughter. The older man stares resolutely at the horizon, ignoring the glacial splendour of the mountains making a slow dance above them as the boat ploughs across the lake. It is the first time that Eva has seen her surroundings from the water, but they still fail to work their magic on her. A garlanded prison or a watery grave, she thinks. She turns her gaze into her lap.

"You should look now, bella." The older guard nudges

Eva gently, alerting her to the fact that he has moved very close behind her. "An island as beautiful as you."

"You fancy her, Severino?" One of the young guards sniggers. "Bit young for you, isn't she?"

"Call me sir!" Severino shouts and cuffs the soldier across the ear. Probably a relative, Eva considers.

She focuses on the two little islands of pink and green, impossibly burdened with so many buildings that they threaten to topple into the water. A fortune balances on the two patches of earth emerging from the lake, and not one inch is spared the part it must play.

The larger of the two islands is top heavy at one end with a greying, ornate palace. Even from the water, its floral decorations scream splendour.

Severino pushes the boy aside in order to guide them in between the flotilla lining both sides of the landing stage.

"Is he already here?" asks Eva.

"They are all here." He pulls alongside the landing stage. "They arrived last night."

Men with guns swarm the tiny square that surrounds the port; its one cafe is shuttered up, abandoned under the surge of military power.

The men jump off the boat, leaving Eva to feel her way to dry land on her own. She stoops, holding on to the sides as she walks to the bow, feeling the boat buckle with every step until she reaches the landing stage. The eyes of the many military guards are on her, so she follows the trio, trying to appear as though she has done this journey a hundred times, looking straight ahead, a small smile set across her mouth. The island is so small that she can almost feel it shift under her feet as she trudges along behind them. She follows them through a series of short alleys, all lined with soldiers with guns resting on their hips who look increasingly menacing as she approaches the palace.

Suddenly, the three men plunge down a steep staircase to reach a mournful door, darkened with damp. The Captain bangs three times and it is opened by a boy of no more than twelve in filthy overalls. The boy looks at Eva, gives a smile of uncertain meaning and opens the door wide for her to enter. The men say nothing and start to walk back up the staircase. One of the younger men turns back to look at Eva but the other one nudges him and sniggers. "Fancy her yourself, do you?"

The boy in the doorway gestures to her to follow. Inside the door is a dank courtyard, leading to a large kitchen. Its only windows are in the ceiling and the light is flat and forbidding. This room has never seen the sunshine. As Eva steps inside the room, she is struck by the scents of sumptuous food preparation: the sharp tang of vinegared lamb, burnt, eggy sweetness, baking bread and red wine sauces. Eva has not smelt such opulence since she used to walk past the backdoors of Milanese hotels, where thin kitchen boys, their eyes sunken with exhaustion, sat in the gutter sucking life from cigarettes.

"Another one, eh?" A stooped chef does not look up from his chopping. "Sit over there." He indicates a stool in the corner by the interior door using the outside of his elbow. "They will call for you when they are ready."

At that, the chef resumes his preparations, only looking up to shout at the boy to hurry up or to cuff him in the head when he tries to creep past to collect a lettuce or a knife. Eva sits and watches the dishes accumulate on the long table next to the door. A poached lamb's head with eyes fixed on escape, a jellied fish the size of a man's thigh, bright salads, waxy mousses amid delicately fragranced rolls arranged in a harvest sheaf. Eva tries to memorise every detail to relate to her mother.

All at once, the door bursts open and six waiters dressed in livery from another age march in. The pistachio frills hanging from their wrists threaten to dip into the dishes, but the men give an expert punch of the air with each hand before grabbing a dish in each. With the practised ease of dancers, they line up with their cargo before filing out of the door again.

The last one to leave holds the door ajar with his foot.

"Quick, signorina," he nods to a small figure cowering behind the door. "Go! Before he changes his mind."

A young girl creeps into the kitchen. Her dress, a chestnut silk, is too big for her and she pulls it around her chest like she is holding herself together. Her face is pale and paths of tears finger her cheeks. Eva jumps to her feet at the sight of the girl's distress.

"Are you alright?" she asks, but the girl turns away from her in horror. Her shoes slap against the stone floor as she stumbles to the outer door as though she has failed to do them up properly in her haste to leave.

The chef does not look at the girl but, once the heavy door has closed behind her, he rolls his eyes in the direction of the boy, who is now washing up the bowls and saucepans at a large sink.

"So now it is lunchtime!" The chef addresses no one in particular. "Always the same."

"What do you mean?" Eva's heart is beating fast. "Who is that girl? What is wrong with her?"

"Keep your questions to yourself, signorina," He wipes his hands on a grimy towel and stretches his hand through the window to retrieve a large pat of butter from a filthy water barrel. "Let us just say that, on these important occasions, not everyone is up to the job."

At his words, Eva feels the weight of the occasion almost overwhelming her. Mussolini himself is here, meeting with the heads of State of Great Britain and France. It is true, she reflects uneasily, that everybody needs to get it right on such a day. What mistakes can the girl have made? A dropped glass? A coughing fit at the wrong moment? Eva hopes to God that she will not make any errors when her time comes.

But when will that be?

The chef and the boy are now assembling the second stage of the meal on the preparation table. Fondant cherries lay deep in a chocolate torte, layers of cream and custard reveal glimpses of orange fruit in a shallow, cut glass trifle bowl. Sweetmeats, cut into neat squares and garlanded with spun sugar, are lined up in rows as regular as toy soldiers.

No more than twenty minutes after they disappeared, the row of waiters bursts through the door again, laden with dirty plates and dishes and an array of cutlery and glasses, which they dump on the wooden board by the sink, where the boy draws them silently into the water.

They gather the desserts and sweetmeats and dissolve through the door in a flurry of frills.

As the chef sighs and pulls out a packet of cigarettes,

the door opens again. Eva gasps as she recognises Stephen. His face is red and his breathing shallow. When he sees her, his eyes widen before he checks himself.

"Did she come this way?" He fails to disguise a panic in his voice.

"Who are you talking about?" she replies.

"A young girl. Brown dress. Crying."

"Yes." Eva keeps her voice calm. She cannot help wanting to challenge him, even in this matter. "She left. Just a few minutes ago."

He looks at her now, as though for the first time, with a growing horror spreading across his face.

"And you… Jesus, what are you doing here?" he gasps.

"Well, I could ask the same of you."

He hesitates, then takes a breath.

"I am filming for a newsreel." He waves his hand towards the upper floors like it was nothing. "You know, history in the making and all that."

Eva keeps her voice steady.

"I, too, am here in an official capacity."

Stephen's face is unreadable. "I think you should go home. Now."

"Don't be ridiculous. I am going nowhere until my business is completed."

"I'm telling you. Get out of here. It is not safe for you."

Then, it dawns on her. He is talking about what he is really doing here. He is planning something. And he does not want her to see it.

But why should he want to protect her? He has only ever been unfriendly, even hostile, during the short time they have been together.

In which case, the only explanation is that he is afraid that she will spoil his plans, whatever they might be. They must involve these heads of state, three world leaders capable of changing history, of either preserving peace, or bringing hundreds, no, thousands of people to the brink.

"Jesus!" Stephen exclaims again and storms back out of the doorway.

The chef and the boy exchange a look that shows only contempt for everyone in this blasted palace.

CHAPTER 10

The call comes as the empty dessert plates and bowls are paraded through the door like war trophies. Eva is still pondering the meaning of Stephen's words when yet another guard, this one in livery bearing the Borromeo emblem, bustles through the waiters looking for her.

"Oh, thank God," he says when he spots her in the corner. "Lunch is over, sweetheart," he recites, "so you're on."

Eva has no time to wonder what use her linen will be to them, now that lunch is over. Maybe they are staying for dinner. The guard continues to beckon furiously until she stands and follows him through the door and up a wide stone staircase, lit by tiny barred windows offering glimpses of the gilded water surrounding the palace. A trio of men stand sentry at the top of the staircase, one of whom opens another door on to the most beautiful room Eva has ever seen. She lets her eyes become accustomed to the light which floods in from so many windows, stacked on top of each other towards a celestial domed ceiling bathed in white and pale blue circular panels. She hears the door snap behind her and turns to see that the doorway has completely disappeared into the wall itself, a trick of clever painting and planning. Crisp white cornicing and statuettes adorn every corner of the room, which would be diamond-shaped, except that a large, circular recess billows from each corner. High up on the walls, a delicate wrought iron balcony sweeps its circle around the whole room. Its serenity seems to hum within the delicate blue walls, enhanced by the lack of furniture, although Eva longs to sit for hours here and breathe in its beauty for herself. A soldier stands at a door in each corner, their brutish firearms seeming quite out of place in this haven. Surely such beauty, even in a building, is a gift from God for everybody, Eva feels. It should not be guarded.

Then she remembers Stephen. Yes, there is danger lurking here. The most important man in Italy is in this very building. Who knows what Stephen has planned? She resolves to look out for Marco so that she can tell him about her concerns, especially if she sees Stephen acting suspiciously again.

She runs to catch up with the Borromeo guard who is striding towards the far door. He whispers something to the soldier, who looks towards Eva and then opens the door to admit them, before looking down at his feet as they tread past.

The next room is a long corridor, its walls heavy with gilt-framed paintings of every size: portraits, some as tiny as postage stamps, others are broad landscapes with privileged figures staring out. The faces of saints, noblemen and women, even devils peer at her with a mute interest. Eva starts to feel the weight of her mission. What if Mussolini does not like her work? What if she, too, says or does the wrong thing?

At one side of the corridor, she spies through an open door what is left of the banquet dishes sprawled on a gold table, being picked at gingerly by what must be the children of the staff, ghostly waifs with blue veins pushing against their thin complexions. Their eyes snap to hers and their fingers speed to their mouths, as though she might represent the end of their puny meal. She hesitates a moment to smile at them, and then trots after the guard, who looks straight ahead to the end of the passage, where he turns swiftly right.

Around this corner, there is another heavily portraited room, lit at both ends by arching windows, whose brilliant, glittering vistas make the art on show look almost pitiful. Here, scattered in little groups, are soldiers dressed in uniform of the same colour as Marco wore last night. She scans them for his tall figure and spots him in the far corner, standing aloof, hunched over with space-staring eyes, although his face is directed at a portrait of a nobleman on a horse.

"Marco," she whispers above the soft hum of men's voices.

As Marco turns towards her voice, the man who has been accompanying her through the palace takes hold of her arm. She reacts to his pinching fingers and jumps away from the door that he has opened into yet another room, just as she glimpses the red and gold of yet another luxurious interior, but this one is darker, womb-like in its reposed softness.

Marco must have seen how roughly he guard handles her. He moves towards Eva, alarm twisting his features.

"It's alright, Marco," she moves towards him, with a holding finger presented to the other guard. "It is just time for my appointment. But I wanted to—"

"Stop!" Marco shouts, and pulls his gun from the holster that is hidden under his short jacket. As all faces swivel round to see who he is aiming at, Eva realises that he is pointing the gun at her.

"What?" she gasps, instinctively drawing her arms around her chest, as though she can stop a bullet by force of will.

"Silence!" screams Marco, his voice thin with something like malice. Two or three others have now drawn their weapons, arching around their colleague with their heads poised like wild dogs. Eva recognises Severino, the older guard who accompanied her on the boat. His expression is an unreadable mix of shock, disappointment and elation at seeing a drama at last.

"What's happening?" she appeals to the Captain, but she falls suddenly sideways as somebody punches her chin. As she tumbles to the floor, she tries to make out whether it is Marco who has struck her. Even before her hand reaches for the pain, she is working out how to take her revenge on him.

"You bastard!" she hisses. "You—"

"This woman is a spy." Marco speaks with the confidence of someone just promoted for hitting a woman. "She was at the Dopolavoro last night taking notes. She poses a danger to Il Duce."

Despite their approval, still the band of men seem

unsure what to do. Eva looks from one to the other. Surely one of them knows her, or her mother, from the village? But even if one recognises her, they do not dare to contradict a man who has so obviously enjoyed his recent work. Instead, it is Severino who comes to her defence.

"Hey, soldier. You have got to be kidding. She is just a girl! "

"She is from Milan." Eva almost laughs to hear this scant justification for the treatment she has received. "I have evidence that she is involved in the suspicious death in Cannero a few days ago, and she has been seen communicating with key suspects in our current investigations. I have no doubt whatsoever that she poses a danger to Il Duce." He pauses a moment and looks around. Finding two young men behind him, he says, "Gianfranco. Salvatore. Take her down to the dungeons while I inform my superiors that we have our suspect at last."

The two men grab her from the floor by her armpits and lead her towards the door through which she entered. Before she is pulled through the doorway, she turns back to see Mussolini, dressed in a soft grey silk robe, poking his bald head through the door of the red-gold room. His eyes are wide with curiosity and his cheeks a rising red. Their eyes meet for a second, then, as she turns away in shame, she hears the door slam with the force of a guillotine.

CHAPTER 11

Once Eva's eyes blink open, she wonders how she can be breathing underwater. It takes a few seconds for her to realise that the undulating lines of light bouncing against the gloom are not water but its reflection. Three small windows illuminate the dungeon from high up one wall. They throw just enough light to discern that walls, ceiling and floor are covered in shells that have been pressed, dome uppermost into a muddy paste to form a surface that is both uneven and unnerving. The dark, decaying layers of shells are relieved only by childish stripes of chalky waves picked out in plaster. The effect is deathlike rather than nautical.

How long has she been asleep, she wonders? Then the events of her recent waking hours come flooding back. Surely, she did not fall asleep after such an ordeal? Which means that she was put to sleep. The horror overwhelms her and she totters to her feet, her legs numbed to their unfolding, her brain coming to life at the same speed.

Marco.

She vaguely remembers being taken down some dingy staircases, the light disappearing as her liberty, and her consciousness, was enfolded in darkness.

But Marco.

She remembers every word he said in the room with the golden portraits. He accused her of being a spy. And a suspect in the murder enquiry.

Her throat thickens with hatred, preventing her from issuing the scream that builds inside her.

Instead, she hurls herself against a thick, iron-riveted door and bangs her fists against it until she sees blood seeping from her knuckles. The sight brings Marco's first blow rushing back to her and she pulls from the door to feel her chin and jaw, checking bones and teeth. All are still intact, but this does nothing to assuage her murderous anger.

How could he have formed such an opinion of her between the Dopolavoro and this morning? If it is still today, even? She has no idea how long she has lain in this prison, although her joints tell her it is more than a few hours. She strains her neck to see out of the brightest of the three windows but she can see only a stretch of blue sky, nothing indicating the time of day or how much time has passed while she has been unconscious on the damp floor.

She runs again to the door, this time able to give the time-honoured cry of the prisoner, despite her film education having taught her its futility.

"Let me out!" she screams. Besides a faint echo issuing through the thick wood, there is, as she expects, no reply.

A second's glance around this dimly-lit room confirms

that there will be no escape. The walls are thick and solid. The door betrays the marks of several locks on the other side.

She slumps against the wall and tries to focus on what might happen now.

If anyone listens to Marco, and, judging by the reactions of his cohort, they certainly seem ready to do so, she will be here until she is transported to the mainland for either questioning or instant imprisonment, depending on how much wine the chief of police has consumed by the time she gets there. If she is lucky enough to be interrogated, can she convince them of her innocence? No doubt, they have, by now, found Amelia's letter tucked under the linens in her bag. She knows they will be thinking the worst of the indecipherable words. After all, she herself had thought it was Russian. At least she knows that the code is impossible to crack. No matter what Amelia found out from her host, the secret is safe for now.

But that does not excuse the fact that she had a coded message in her bag. Add that solid piece of evidence to whatever lies Marco has manufactured and these vindictive guards have more than enough reason to take this further. Or to leave her in here forever.

She wonders whether they will give her anything to eat or drink. There is a filthy pot in the corner for her to relieve herself but this provides little reassurance. Again, her thoughts return to Marco. What on earth has caused him to turn against her?

The only answer is that in between last night, when he touchingly escorted her back to her front door, leaving with a respectful goodbye, and this morning, he has discovered something that has linked her to Stephen. Could someone have spotted her in the woods? Did they see her handle the gun? Or could the doorman at the hotel in Luino have alerted the authorities after she was asking questions about the Englishman? None of these suspicions seem outrageous. She has heard many similar tales, ending usually in arrest. She should have been more careful in her words and actions. She scolds herself enough to make her body double over in self-admonishment. The imagined words of her mother or Amelia are hardly needed.

The sound of footsteps on the stairway outside the door makes her sit up and wipe away her tears. She readies herself for the arrival of the guards, eager to administer some rough justice. After a few troubled turns of rusty locks, the door swings open and one of the uniformed mob pushes open the door. She does not recognise him.

Behind him shuffles a hooded shape in brown sackcloth, who, once the guard has left and shut the door on them again, reveals himself to be Padre Giacomo. Despite his obvious pleasure at setting eyes on Eva again, he maintains a sombre expression as he blesses her with his right hand.

"My poor girl. How did this ever happen?"

Eva cannot think of a suitable response to this and, in her gratitude that she is in the presence of a priest rather than a thug, she rushes to hug him, remembering just in time to drop to her knees in a remorseful curtsey.

"Now, my child… there is no need for that." He hauls her to her feet and gives her a second blessing. "You have got yourself in one hell of a mess but you should be thankful: somebody is watching over you." His eyes lift to the ceiling and she realises with a start why he is here. Why a priest would be sent to a prisoner's cell. He is going to help her make her peace with God before she is executed. Tears come quickly to her eyes and her first thought is for her mother. The second for her father. He, too, died at the behest of the Italian regime, and with no more justification than this ridiculous sentence that is being laid down for her. Her cold fear transforms into a resigned, hot anger.

The priest is searching in his voluminous pockets. She imagines that he will pull out a cross to bless her with or a rosary for them to recite together.

"What's the point, Father?" She tries to still his searching hands with hers. "You cannot save me from this and God has clearly abandoned me or I would not be facing my death today."

The priest hardly seems to hear her as he finds what he is looking for with a grunt of relief. He finally looks up at her crumpled face as he starts to tug out a navy piece of cloth. She cannot understand the beginnings of a smile on his face as he holds up a convent wimple. Eva almost laughs at him. Surely, he is not asking her to take holy orders and become a nun? Can he really be imposing such demands now? Does a zealot lurk beneath the priest's drunken, lax style of Catholicism.

"Don't be afraid, my child." He holds the wimple towards her. "Put this on and we can leave this place."

"I am not putting it on!" Eva pulls away from him and presses back against the slimy wall. "If they are going to kill me, they can look at me just as I am, not in a ridiculous religious costume. They can look at my hair, my eyes, and they can decide if killing a young girl is what passes for morality these days."

"Eva!" He holds crucifixion palms towards her. "Why are you talking about killing? I have come to take you home."

"What?" She greets this news with as much doubt as when he lied about seeing Stephen yesterday. He is either a fool or a fantasist. "How can I go home? I have been accused of spying."

"Eva, I am not supposed to reveal how or why to you. But let's say that a few thousand lire go a long way…" He lifts the wimple over her head and pulls it around her shoulder where it hangs like a noose. "I am only supposed to accompany my new nun out of this palace and down to the boat that is waiting at the port, in which we will return to Cannero."

"But who has told you to do this? Marco called me a spy in front of all those guards. And he— " She cannot bring herself to say what he did to her. A deep shame at putting her trust in him, even while she herself deceived him, throttles her words.

"All in good time, Eva." He clasps her arm and bangs on the door three times. "But now, for your own safety, come with me and say nothing."

The guard opens the door and they file past him without a word. An instinct tells Eva to bow her head, but the guard is looking back into the cell, as though the real Eva has remained there. The priest does not let go of her arm as they climb two more flights of stairs. Their progress is slowed by his increasingly heavy breathing. Eva can smell the outdoor air before they reach it, danger has sharpened her senses. They reach a heavy door that stands open; beyond it is a shadowed stairwell. Her head fills with questions, then a deep terror that they will be intercepted by someone who will recognise her beneath this feeble disguise.

They scuttle through the gloomy alleys towards the sound of the boats that are still coming and going from the dock. How long since she disembarked here, she wonders? When they reach the square, the light makes her blink and retract but the priest continues to pull her towards a small wooden boat tied to the side of the dock. He climbs down a ladder and plops into it, making it rock in the water. She waits for the waves to subside and she steps into the boat and sits down beside him with her eyes closed. He turns to start up the motor and its roar makes her start and look upwards to the crowds on the bank. She thinks she sees Marco in the sea of faces. He is looking at her but she cannot read his expression, either. It is as though everyone wears a mask today.

She stares at the edge of the lake as the priest manoeuvres the boat around the island. She can hardly bear to look at the little islands now, with their bulging buildings suffocating their natural beauty. The sun shoots its rays off the water as normal. For the first time, Eva finds she can look into its depths. Under the surface of the water is another world, she thinks, free from the horrors that humans generate with such ease. She pulls off her wimple and feels her hair snap in the wind.

Paola is waiting on the harbour, Eva climbs out of the boat at Cannero. Her mother's whole body is stooped in a near parody of worry and woundedness.

"Where have you been, Eva?" Paola's tone is shrill

but her grip is yielding as she hugs Eva close to her body. "Padre Giacomo said that you had been delayed but he could not say why. I have been frantic with worry."

"Let us go back to the house and I will try to explain, Mama. It was just a misunderstanding."

Eva pulls herself away from her mother's grasp and takes her arm to pull her up towards the path leading to their road.

"Not until you have shown your gratitude to the Padre, Eva."

Eva lets out a sharp breath and struts back down the path to the Padre, who has been staring after them.

She holds out her hand, after checking that her mother is watching from far enough way that she will not hear her words.

"Thank you, Padre, for bringing me home." He shakes her hand and bends his head towards her.

"Come and see me tomorrow, my child," he murmurs. "I can't tell you, I'm unable to tell you… but there is something else I need to say."

Before she can reply, he has turned away in the opposite direction towards the church, pulling his cowl over his head as he hurries past the cafes. It is only then that she realises that her bag, with Amelia's letter and all the samples, has not been returned to her.

CHAPTER 12

It had been easier than she expected to allay her mother's fears. Eva soon learned that she had spent nearly twenty-four hours in the cell but she must have slept during most of it because, rather than exhaustion, she feels full of energy. By the following morning, her anger and anxiety has turned to pure adrenalin.

Her mother seems to accept Eva's explanation: that she was arrested on suspicion of spying. Such things happen all the time, Paola says, so let us be thankful that they realised their mistake. She reassures Eva that they must have sent Padre Giacomo to accompany her as she made her exit because it was easier than issuing an order for the guards streaming over the island to allow her free passage.

Paola is less willing to blame only Marco for the incident, however.

"Yes, he is a bruto, and I will never welcome him, or any of his family, into my house again. But what could you have done to make him say such a thing?"

Eva says nothing about her questions at the Dopolavoro,

or about Stephen's presence at Borromeo. She must lie low until all this has blown over. No more questions, no more amateur sleuthing. Full-bodied fascism, with all its paranoia and prejudice, has now reached even the tranquil villages of the paradise that is Lake Maggiore. Hopefully, it is not too late to sink under the fascists' radar and lead the quiet life that Paola encourages.

When Paola seems sufficiently calm, Eva leaves her sewing. "You are right," she says. "I must have given the wrong impression to Marco."

Paola looks up with an admiring smile. "That is good, Eva. You are learning humility."

"Yes, mother." Eva pulls her shawl about her. "So I am going to make my confession. Padre Giacamo said that it would help clear my conscience so that I could get on with my life."

"That is good," Paola repeats, before turning back to her sewing.

Eva walks out into the fresh, clear morning, and takes a deep breath. Instead of turning up the hill towards the forest, she skips down towards the harbour, where she spies Scimmia, making his usual surveillance of the fishing nets. As though no time has passed at all, the little dog trots into step behind Eva, who turns under the arch on to the esplanade, where the same tourists study the timetable at the boarding post, and hover between cafes deciding which will most satisfy their desires. She gazes out across the water to the mountains beyond the lake, where a dusting of snow balances on their tips like a flimsy hat.

She turns the corner on to Amelia's road and halts suddenly. Three official-looking cars are pulled up outside the palazzo. Military vehicles, perhaps, but then two liveried porters emerge from the front gate laden with leather trunks and ornate cases, which they pile into the boot of one of the cars before returning for more.

Amelia must be leaving. She might be going back to England, or continuing with the Grand Tour. Either way, it is goodbye. Eva squeezes past the cars and walks through the gardens to the front door, which hangs open.

"Mi scusi?" she calls into the hall, in an assertive mezzo forte, hoping that a servant will emerge to take her to Amelia.

Instead, a tall man dressed in tweed comes down the staircase. His leisurely speed perfectly matches his languid manner.

Without looking in her direction, he starts opening drawers in the ornate hall stand, an array of parasols, fishing nets and walking sticks all trying to get in his way.

"Damn and blast!" he splutters, as a picnic basket falls from the top of the stand, splaying its contents around his feet.

Finally, he notices Eva and looks at her, exasperated at another interruption.

"Can I help you?" She is not surprised that he makes no attempt at speaking Italian. "Cook's still in the kitchen and the servant's entrance is round the back." He indicates a route back out through the front door and right turn with military hands.

"I am looking for… I am a friend of Amelia's."

He studies her more closely, as if trying to work out in what circumstances Amelia could possibly have befriended a local.

"Miss Granger is leaving." He turns back to continue his search. "If I can just find these damn keys, we'll be on our way even sooner."

"I thought she said... a week at least."

"Calm down, Miss..."

"Eva."

"Ah yes, she told me about you." He stopped his busy fingers and turned to face her. "The one with the interest in Englishmen."

"No, I..."

"Don't worry, Eva, I won't tell anyone. No need to look so scared; I am not kidnapping her. There is no subterfuge here. I am taking Miss Granger and the two old crones to my house in Paris. It is getting a bit too hot here, and I don't mean the weather. Everyone's in Paris at the moment, anyway."

"Of course," Her English teacher in Milan had taught her to use this phrase in order to allow her to agree with the disagreeable. "But this is very sudden?"

"Lightning strikes. Lightning strikes, Eva." His face lights up as if remembering a good dinner. "I couldn't stop myself. I asked her just last night and she agreed."

"Agreed to what?"

"To be my wife! What, she didn't mention me to you?" Eva thinks back to the fear that had crossed Amelia's face when she thought she would be discovered by this man.

"No, sir, she didn't. But... she must be very happy. Congratulations to you both. Can I see her?"

"Well, she is a bit busy currently, as we want to get out of here before nightfall. But I can give her a message for you, if you like."

His face is smiling but his legs are planted in a wide stance across the base of the staircase. She has only one way to turn.

"Can you give her this?" She pulls the copy of *Murder on the Orient Express* out of her bag and hands it to him.

"Ah, so this is where you have been cooking up all your ideas about Stephen?"

"Yes," she smiles awkwardly. "Just silly girlish fantasies. If you could give it back to her with my thanks, I would be grateful."

"Fantastic!" He pulls a set of keys out of a drawer and, before he bangs it shut, places the book inside. "Now, we can get going." He looks at Eva as though it is the first time he has noticed her. "Er... Is there anything else?"

"No, sir." She wrings her hands. "But, Amelia mentioned that you knew Stephen quite well, and the drowned boy. Before you go, would you mind telling me how you met?"

"So you are interested in Englishmen?" He turns a wide smile in her direction. "If only I had known before... we could have had some fun. But Stephen and Sam would have been no use to you."

Sam. At last, she has a name.

"No use at all to an ambitious Italian girl looking to land herself a husband and a passport. Stephen is itching to get back to Blighty to see his wife... And Sam, well, you know what happened to him..."

"Not really, sir. All I know is that he is dead."

"Yes, all over some nasty business in Luino. Quite ridiculous, really."

Eva remains quiet, waiting for him to betray Sam's

ecrets. She has only known Amelia a couple of days, but already she senses that this man will do nobody any good in life, especially not a wife.

"I told him at the time to leave the girl alone, brat or no brat."

Brat. She has not heard the word before. She racks her brains for similar words to help her translate. Bright. Rat. She cannot ask this brute of a man. She needs to ask Amelia.

"Can I get in touch with Amelia? Where will you be staying in Paris?"

"Oh, I have no idea," He starts to walk towards the front door, ushering her out. "Maybe The Metropole, or The Colonnade. Depends on where a penthouse is available. Really, is it so urgent? I can pass a message on if you like? I am sure she will write to you, if she…"

Eva thinks quickly. "Do you have pen and paper?"

He rifles in another drawer and takes out some sheets of vellum — the same paper that Amelia used for her notes. It takes Eva a while to compose her words, using the remembered line from Agatha Christie as a key.

SORRY I HAVE NOT RETURNED YOUR BOOK. PLEASE TELL ME WHAT IS A 'BRAT'? CONGRATULATIONS ON YOUR MARRIAGE. YOUR FRIEND, EVA.

She folds the note into quarters to give it to Amelia's fiancé, who must think she is illiterate since it has taken her so long to write it. As he takes it from her, she hears the rush of footsteps coming down the stairs and her eyes are drawn upwards to the arrival of Amelia, dressed in cream linen, a clinging bonnet framing her elfin face.

Amelia's look of joy is quickly replaced with reserve when she sees Eva and her fiancé standing in the hallway.

"But John!" she coos, "Why did you not tell me that Eva was here?"

"She can't stay, anyway." He turns and almost pushes Eva out of the front door. "She was just leaving this note for you."

Amelia ignores him, pushing past to embrace her friend. She switches to Italian. "Did you get mine yesterday? What did you think?"

"I haven't read it. I am afraid I… lost it." The thought of embarrassing both herself and her friend with the tale of her arrest and imprisonment in front of this man is unthinkable.

"Well, I suppose you have already heard." She darts a meaningful look at her fiancé. "About John and me."

"Yes, I heard. Many congratulations. So sudden and, of course, romantic."

"Yes, isn't it?" Amelia has regained her look of the newly engaged. "But the note was really to give you my address in England. Well, where my mother lives, so that we can stay in touch. Because I want to hear all about the…" She darts another look at John. "Well, how you are getting on here?"

"Please write it down for me, Amelia," she hands her a piece of paper and the pen, "so that I can tell you all about it."

Amelia scribbles something on the paper and crumples it into Eva's hand.

"Sorry that we are in such a rush, darling." She kisses Eva on both cheeks. "So much to do."

And Amelia is gone. Eva walks back down the path and spots Scimmia sitting in the back of the car, a shining blue ribbon around his neck.

Five minutes later, Eva is back on the esplanade, clutching Amelia's note. She thinks about her friends in Milan. All they had really wanted, despite all the bravado and the insults hurled at the young boys, was to land a husband. For a brief day or two, she has thought that Amelia was different. But now she has been deserted by her new friend. She understands now why she has never before trusted a woman: no matter how devoted she is, a woman will always leave you for a man. All the clothes, the make-up, the beauty — they are all directed to one outcome. So why should she be surprised, let alone upset? The supposed security of a romantic relationship trumps friendship every time.

More fool her that she thought Amelia was different…

Heaving a sigh, she uncrumples Amelia's note and finds two addresses on it. One is for an address in a place called Mayfair in London, the other is for an art gallery in Luino.

CHAPTER 13

It seems like at least a month, a year even, since she climbed this hill to the church. It is now approaching the middle of the day and the sun beats down on her shoulders and back, stiffening her blouse. Even the craziest tourist knows to stay out of this, but Eva feels a pride in weathering her native heat. Besides, the church beckons, offering both cool air and possibly even some answers. She is excited to run through her questions in her head. Maybe after a day, Padre Giacomo will have more to say on how he came to rescue her. And how much does he know about Stephen? And how did Stephen get word to him to come and get her from the shell-dungeon? She is in no mood to let him evade these questions. With every hour that passes, she feels angrier at how she is being treated, ignored, kept in the dark, like a child who cannot handle the truth. Still, unravelling such a mystery will take more than a few words from a priest.

She can hear a choir of young boys singing the fascist

anthem, Giovinezza, as the path hovers above the roof of the primary school and she thinks back to the last time she heard it with Amelia. "Youth is beautiful," they sing, but their voices are hard and thin. She has never had what her mother calls 'a skin sister', a friend she can tell everything to and who knows what she is thinking before she says anything. Giovanna in Milan was the closest friend she'd had, but some reticence in Eva had found Giovanna looking to other girls for her heart-to-hearts. That moment with Amelia had given Eva a glimpse of what a good friend could mean, how she could change the colour of the passing days in Cannero. The glance they shared, she realises now, was an invitation to a new society, one where Mussolini's fascism and his hard rules governing what women can and cannot do, is a thing of the past. She did not need an English girl to show her another way of life, but it seems strange that it was Amelia, and not one of the factory girls who think of nothing but marriage, to whom she was drawn.

The bell of the town clock announces a quarter to twelve as she pushes open the heavy door. It is well known that Giacomo is found at the taverna by noon, beginning his public inebriation. She does not have much time. Maybe the lack of time will help his tongue loosen.

The air is thick with musty incense and Eva blinks before becoming accustomed to the gloom. There is nobody to be seen in the church, although the air is at least ten degrees cooler. She hears the door at the far end, the one leading to the Padre's apartments, close with a gentle thud; Giacomo must have let himself out. The burning candles suggest that he has not yet left for his midday aperitif. Eva sits down to wait. She studies the beams of light piercing through the dust of the windows on the right-hand side of the church. Nothing will keep out the sun.

Suddenly, the Padre pulls open the faded curtain of the confessional, a grey wooden box tucked under the cold stone eaves. She jumps as he steps out and beckons her over. Before she has time to consider who could have been slipping through the back exit from the church, he calls her name.

"Your mother told me you would come," he drools. "Although you are a little later than I expected. Where have you been?"

"I walked along the front to the factory," she replies, thinking quickly. "I had promised to lend one of the girls my embroidered scarf."

He seems to accept this explanation, only allowing himself a small expression of disappointment. Not for the first time, Eva despairs at the close relationship her mother still seems to cherish with this over-pious drunk. What on earth has she in common with him? Her mother is godly, but her beliefs have a certain practicality.

He disappears back behind his curtain and pulls it shut. The curtain on the other side of the divide hangs open, waiting for her. Eva has always dreaded entering the confessional, as though God could see into her very soul as soon as she kneels down and starts praying. The Padre would be thrilled if he knew the power that the ritual of confessing her sins held over her but she refuses to let him see her fear. She stomps into the box and has barely pulled the curtain back in place behind her before she starts reciting her prayers.

"Bless me, father, for I have——"

"Eva, I need to talk to you."

His words stop her breath. She looks up at the screen which divides them but the dark shadows that hover around its carved shapes give nothing away. She listens for his rasping breath but can hear nothing. It is as though he has been replaced by a different person. Even the smell of alcohol has gone.

"What?"

"There is no time for explanations, Eva. I do not know how much time I have."

Is he ill? Or is he, too, under threat from the authorities?

"I cannot answer the questions I am sure you have. I know you wish to know how I came to rescue you from the Palace, but I assure you I have no more to say on the matter, for your own sake. No, it is about another matter I need to speak to you."

Eva puts her ear closer to the screen. She can feel his breath starting to quicken.

"As you know, I am very close to your mother. We have worked… I mean, we have spoken often since you both arrived here. She has told me something that I think it is important that you know."

Eva opens her eyes wide. There is so much she wants to know. Why have they come to Maggiore? Where is the rest of their family? Why does she feel so different from other girls her age?

She senses the Padre's hesitation with the horror of watching a friend slip off the edge of a cliff.

"What is it, Padre? Is it about my liberation from Borromeo? Did she do something to——"

141

"I cannot tell you what it is. But you must—"

"What? What are you saying? Why are you playing with me like this—"

"I cannot tell you, Eva, simply because Paola told me this in the confessional. You know that what is said in here is sacrosanct and cannot be divulged to anyone, not even to the police."

At the mention of the police, Eva's mind starts racing. What has her mother got involved with? All Paola's talk of keeping Eva safe, pulling her away from Milan in order to come to this backwater, was it all just a smokescreen to mask her own activities? She resolves to keep her suspicions to herself, however.

"I understand, of course, Father."

"That is good," his breathing settles back to normal. "But the impact of her secret on you is profound. Quite profound. If only I could…" Eva hears his voice breaking.

"What can I do, Father?"

"You must speak to her. I won't be here much longer, I am sure. When I am gone, you must tell her that you have spoken to me and that you wish to know the truth."

Then he slips from the confessional. By the time Eva has pulled back the curtain, there is no sign of him.

§

On her way back up to the apartment, Eva spies her neighbour, Signora Catalino. She can just make out her silhouette bent in ardent prayer, her window cloaked in Spanish black lace.

Opening the front door, Eva steps into darkness,

drawn to a single candle that lights Paola's head, bending over her work and Eva sees the reds and greens of the Christmas holly. A wave of frustration washes over Eva. Why does she spend her time creating these baubles for the rich, when their own lives are so difficult? There has to be something they can do that is more worthwhile.

Paola looks up.

"You have seen the priest?"

"Yes, I have. He had some interesting things to say."

Paola's head twists imperceptibly. "Really?" Eva watches Paola force herself to look back at her sewing.

"He said I needed to talk to you urgently. About something of vital importance."

Her words hang in the air like a threatening cloud. Finally, Paola puts down her sewing.

"I can't imagine why he has decided to bring you into our confidence now." She sighs. "Our business is almost concluded. There is really nothing that you can do to help. Except maybe keep out of the eye of the authorities. For once."

"But mother! I have done nothing but go and look for buyers for our work! I can't explain what happened to me on Borromeo any more than Scimmia can!"

"No, but something happened. And whatever it was, whatever Marco saw and decided to act upon, we are now exposed to the authorities in a way that we never were before." The finger of guilt pointed at Eva is almost visible.

"But... if we keep ourselves to ourselves for a while and arouse no further suspicion, won't they forget all about us? What harm can they think we are capable of? Two women on their own in a strange town?"

Paola stares at her daughter as though she hardly recognises her. "Well. I thought no matter what mistakes I was guilty of in raising you up on my own, or in taking you away from your friends and bringing you here to a new town, I never thought that I would hear you say that women are not capable — of harm, or good, or otherwise."

Eva's mouth opens as she gulps for air with which to grasp this statement of her mother's. Has she gone mad? This advocate of women as mothers, homemakers and carers and nothing more — what is she saying? Can somebody change so drastically in a matter of hours?

"For God's sake! Two days ago you told me that only a fascist son-in-law could protect me! Are you feeling alright, Mother?" She resists the impulse to cry. Instead, she would like to turn around and run, run to Amelia's house and climb in the car with Scimmia to go to Paris, or England, or anywhere, with her and her fiancé.

"Sit down, Eva." Paola has risen, swiped her work to the floor with one hand and pulled out a chair. Eva knows to obey without a word. Once she is seated, Paola pulls another chair directly opposite.

"Eva. My darling." She sighs and Eva feels her fears ignite.

"I was not going to tell you any of this until we were living in safer times, but, from what you say, Giacomo seems to feel that, not only are you ready for the information, but that you may be able to help us in some way."

And out it comes. A story to throw everything Eva thought she knew about her own mother on its head. About Paola the radical, who takes messages, pressed deep into her swathes of embroidery, to the partisans living in

144

the hills. Who secures passports for people who face real threats from the fascists. Who, together with Giacomo, helps to smuggle Liberals, anti-fascists and, more recently, Jewish people out of the country, over the mountains and into Switzerland. Eva, to whom this story should have been a fairytale, feels strangely nauseous at the thought of her mother doing the kinds of things that she should have been doing, except she has chosen to dream of the glitter of Hollywood.

"But why didn't you tell me?" Eva's voice is unrecognisable, thin like a seagull's cry. "You... you are all I have in the world. And it has all been a lie."

"But don't you see? We couldn't risk it." She silences Eva's protests with raised hands. "You have always been so... I don't know... romantic. I know you wanted me to be a better person, but I had to be somebody else, or I could not have been able to do my real work. What better camouflage than a drunk priest and a pious widow? We have aroused not a single shred of suspicion." She narrows her eyes, "Until now."

"You told me to go to Commissario Bianchi if I saw the Englishman again! I would have walked into the lion's den and you would have watched me do it!"

"Bianchi is with us, Eva. It is he who tells us when somebody is in danger and we set to work."

Eva is finally able to think of her own interests. "Is that why we came here? Why we had to leave Milan? Weren't there enough opportunities for your... rebellion... there?"

Paola drops her eyes to her lap. "Eva, I..."

"What is it? What happened there?" Her voice becomes shrill. "Were we in danger? Is that why we left so suddenly?"

"Eva. Stop this." Paola face has become ashen. "I cannot answer those questions. Not now. There is not enough time." She sighs again and presses her lips together, as though there is something she longs to confess to her own daughter. "All I can say is that we are safer here. Nobody suspects us and, until yesterday, we were able to conduct our activities without any suspicion. Yes, maybe I kept you a child for too long. But I did it for your sake, to keep you safe."

"But it makes no sense. Why would Giacomo want me to know about this now? When I have just been arrested? When I need to keep away from trouble."

"I don't know for sure, my chi—, I mean, my daughter." A final sigh. "I can only imagine that he is thinking of using you as a decoy."

CHAPTER 14

The next day, Eva is awakened before sunrise by a muffled knock on the door.

"Quickly!" hisses Paola, pulling her dress over her nightclothes as she approaches the door. "We don't want to wake up the trout-face below." The use of such a word, along with this nocturnal urgency, adds to Eva's feeling of having aged overnight, a new complicity with a mother who she can, almost, admire.

From behind her curtain, she can hear Giacomo and Paola whispering.

"So, you told her, yes?"

"Well, I had to, after what you said to her. But, once I had got over the shock, I agree that this could be useful for us."

"For us?" He stares at her. Through the gap between the curtain and the wall, Eva sees his eyes pierce through Paola as though he thought she has gone mad.

"Yes, Padre." She reaches for his hand. "I asked you to come this morning, so that we could come up with a plan for her to draw some of the guards away from Stephen. I thought of sending her to Luino. After all, she knows it reasonably well after her last trip. She could—"

"Paola! Think about what are you saying!"

"She will be safe. She has nothing to hide. She can simply visit some of the traders and come home. It will not be dangerous."

"I did not mean this." The way he emphasises the word makes Eva shiver. The memory of the shell dungeon is still dampening her bones.

"Padre! I thought this was what you had planned! You told her about us… about me. What did you expect?"

"I said nothing, Paola. I simply said she should talk to you. I did not mean—"

"Oh, Giacomo. What did you expect? Well, it is too late, now. The rabbit has slipped through la trappola. And I think it is a good idea. There will be little risk for her, and it will help us divert three or four pairs of eyes from Stephen when we start him on his journey."

"Oh, Paola." His tone is mournful, as though it carries the weight of the world, which he is presenting to God in all its horror. It is the first time Eva has heard him sound like a man of the cloth.

"Eh!" Paola shrugs, the way she does to end a conversation. She calls for Eva, who pulls back the cloth. When she approaches the table, her mother's smile is even broader than when she met Marco for the first time.

"Figlia mia, you are not worried about being our little diversion today, are you? I have not trapped you, or blackmailed you, into doing this, have I?"

"Of course not, Mother." Eva kisses her on both

cheeks and sits down opposite the two of them. "Padre."
She nods dutifully to the priest, who sighs and softens his
eyes.

"My child." He extends his hands across the table.
"Although, of course, you are not a child and have not
been for some years now." He looks meaningfully at Paola,
who ignores him. Eva tries to read his meaning. Is she
really in danger? Now she can no longer trust anything
Paola says, it feels like her life, as she knew it, is over. What
has she to lose? If she takes on this task, she may gain
in stature in her mother's eyes. Become an adult, despite
Paola's attempts to keep her as a child all these years.

"What is it you want me to do?"

"That's my girl!" Paola beams and pulls a paper from
the pocket of her overall and studies it. "We are due to
deliver Stephen to his chaperones at midday, so——"

"Stephen?" Eva stiffens. "The Englishman?"

"You have met him, no?"

"I thought it was him who had me arrested at
Borromeo!"

"We thought so, too," Giacomo looks grave. "But he
says he had nothing to do with it. He has his own troubles,
as I will tell you. We, too, thought that he might have
pointed the finger at you in order to divert attention from
himself… but he assures us that he did no such thing."

"But how did you know to come and get me? How did
you fool the guards into letting me escape?"

"I received a letter giving me full instructions where
to go and what to do. I don't know who it was from and
thank God the plan worked. But, still, the facts about your
arrest remain a… a mystery."

"But one that we can turn to our advantage." Paola continues to beam. "Giacomo says that there is a regular trio of guards at the harbour, watching the comings and goings."

"Yes, I… have seen them."

"Good. Then, if we can get them to follow you to Luino somehow, that leaves the way clear for our plan to leave for the border, where the chaperones are waiting to take Stephen to Switzerland."

"To Switzerland? Why, what has he done? And why go at midday? Wouldn't the darkness give a better cover?"

"Ahh, Eva… you have watched too many films, I think."

The priest, repeating one of her mother's favourite sayings, stops her breath. All over again, she is shocked at how close in thinking they are. However, Paola intervenes.

"You are wrong, Padre! It is all that training that makes her perfect for her first task today."

"And what is that? If it is not a secret to be kept from such a shallow, starstruck mind…"

"Stephen will be arriving in an hour when Signora Catalina leaves her flat to go to the market." They are both staring at her intently, as though lives depend on her actions. "We want you to turn him into an Italian."

CHAPTER 15

When Giacomo responds to Stephen's gentle knock at the door, Paola is pouring coffee into scratched yellow, porcelain cups, another of the few relics from Milan. He smiles at Paola and the Padre but Eva finds herself looking away. Here is the man that has been at the heart of all the troubles of the last few days. The man who instructed her to carry out an investigation that she had no appetite for, who drew Amelia under his spell, despite never meeting her, who avoided arrest at Borromeo, only to witness her own shameful incarceration.

She thought he must have been the one who helped free her.

Now, it turns out, he is being protected by her own mother.

This last revelation is the worst betrayal.

While Stephen settles himself at the table and sips his coffee, Eva broods quietly in the corner. Ever since they came to Cannero, she has tried so hard to be the daughter that her mother said she wanted. Dutiful, hard-working, pious. And now it turns out that the mother she tried so hard to please is somebody else entirely.

One of the strangest conundrums that Eva now faces is that, rather than rejoice that she and her mother share the same beliefs, she feels an inexplicable revulsion. In some sense, being opposed to her mother's views fitted her own anger, the anger that she has felt inside ever since… ever since when? For as long as she can remember.

Eva gets up and gestures towards the curtain. "We can leave these two to their plotting." Stephen follows her and sits on the chair she has dragged behind her. He loosens his shirt and breathes solidly, expectantly, his face a mask of uncertainty.

Eva tips out her make-up on to the bed and listens to the familiar clunk of the cartons. Just as she did the night of the wake, she swirls her fingers among the products to hear more of their music. The coral lipstick she bought in Milan, using the proceeds from sewing a thousand tiny pearls on to a wedding dress for the daughter of a Liberal landowner, a powder compact she acquired after completing a pirate's outfit for a little prince's birthday.

She is a little alarmed that the familiar fantasy has not floated into her head — being discovered by a Hollywood film producer, the escape from Italy and inevitable domesticity, and the life of an independent woman among the glamourous circles of Los Angeles. Without giving herself time to grieve, she reaches for a brush.

"Are we aiming for Piedmont, or Sicily?"

"Eva, I am going to Switzerland, and then back to England from there. If God allows, of course…" Stephen smiles at Eva with the indulgence of a parent.

"I know that, Stephen." She grabs his forehead and pulls his hair back into a black scarf. "My question concerns your appearance. Would you like to become a Northern or a Southern Italian?"

"Is there a difference?"

"You have a lot to learn about our people, Stephen."

Feeling herself to have gained more of a balance in their relationship, Eva gets to work.

"You will be a Piedmontese: a merchant who has never spent a day in the fields. Do your new papers indicate an age?"

"I am to be forty."

"What happened to your own passport?"

"It was taken from my hotel. The concierge was keeping it but Commissario Bianchi told your mother that the fascists had requisitioned it in advance of an investigation. That could only spell one thing. I was lucky your mother found me in time or I…"

He drifts into silence, which grows in intensity as she works, as he contemplates what might have been and the dangers of the days ahead.

Eva darkens his hair and ages his skin, weathering it to suggest long, outdoor summers and winters in comfortable apartments with fires and regular hot dinners. She thickens his eyebrows and makes his lips more voluptuous. But she reminds herself, her work has to be invisible, much like her life. This will be her masterpiece, she decides.

It feels like her moving fingers are tracing a farewell to her childish love of artifice, adornment, dreams.

When she finishes, removing the linen she has placed around his shoulders, she surveys her work with the detachment of an embalmer, as though the Stephen she knew, the one that set her mind racing over the mystery of his drowned friend, no longer exists.

"I wish you well, Stephen." She can see that his head is already in the mountains that await him. "But I would like to ask you one more thing before you leave."

"Be my guest, Eva. It is doubtful whether we will ever see each other again."

"I want to ask you about Sam, the man who drowned. You were so angry that first night, so insistent that I right the wrong that had been done to him. My mother has told me that he too was Jewish. But why did you ask me to find the culprit when you knew it was dangerous? I have been assaulted, imprisoned and followed constantly since I first set eyes on you. I deserve an explanation."

"Just forget it, Eva. I am sorry I placed you in danger. It was stupid of me. There is nothing you can do to bring him back and I will be leaving in an hour or two. I suppose I believe that all people, of whatever religion, male or female, have a right to see their family, to bring up their children, no matter how difficult it might seem to others. Promise me that you will remember that when you, eventually, have children."

Eva strains to make sense of his words as Stephen gets up from his seat. What has family and parenthood got to do with Sam's death? His tone is patronising, like he is in a kind of trance. Is it because he is risking death himself in the next few hours?

And the idea that she herself should bring children into this world seems so preposterous that all Eva can do is shrug before her mother comes bustling in through the curtain. Paola smiles at the perfect Italian man she has created.

"It is time," she says.

CHAPTER 16

An hour later, Eva is tiptoeing past her neighbour's window, although her mission is far from secret. In fact, Paola has told her to draw attention to herself as much as she can, even leaving her red hair uncovered. As she walks out of the gate into the alley, her body moves with a maturity, with a purpose that knits together her limbs, giving her body a new poise that is nothing like the swagger of the marriageable girls of the town, or like anything she has seen (and sometimes tried to copy) in Milan.

Instead of turning left towards the port, she pulls the scarf back over her head and turns up the hill and walks through the marketplace, towards the woods. Once inside its whispering darkness, she runs up the path to the tree containing the gun. She glances around to check there is no one there and then reaches in. She is relieved to feel the coarse linen covering over the cold metal. Stephen must have decided that taking it over was reckless. She takes the gun from its hiding place and unwraps it. Her fingers start to shake. But she knows how to check that its bullets are in place from the films she has seen. She presses her thumb on the barrel and it clicks open. There are six gleaming bullets waiting in their slots. Her hands shake more as she slots the barrel back in place and returns the gun to its cloth, finally squeezing it into the bottom of her bag, under her samples.

By the time she reaches the little port, all fear has left her. Each breath has filled her with the essence of her role: a confident spy edging towards breaking the system and protecting an innocent man. When she sees the three guards that accompanied her on her last trip, lolling on the water's edge, eyeing the women who are milling about, and tossing remarks between them about how their husbands must feel, she almost smiles. Can it be this easy to lure away the state's security?

When they spot Eva, they straighten up, nudge each other and then, after a word from the senior guard she recognises as Severino, consciously resume their nonchalant positions, stiff as poor actors in a play.

She manages to avert her eyes; her hair drops across her face as she pulls her purse from her bag and retrieves some coins for the ferry. As she takes her place in the queue, she takes an inventory of her fellow passengers, suddenly fearful that somebody else should today prove more enticing than she. But she finds only tourists, with their shouts battling for supremacy when choosing the day's itinerary.

She collects her ticket and sits on one of the benches, watching, as they all do, the tiny dot that is clinging to Luino's shoreline, waiting for it to grow into the shape of a ferry approaching the bank, that will bring a shape of sorts to their long, aimless day. The guards are watching it, too, talking to each other in low voices, something which they seem to find quite difficult, as Eva can make out some of what they are saying.

"Hang back...," Severino mumbles, "... until the mark makes a move..."

"But I need to be back in time for lunch," one of the younger guards grumbles in reply, "The wife has made pasta a la vongole this time. Is it really worth going to Luino?"

She almost smiles at their pathetic needs, but checks herself, just in time, remembering that these are the men who would happily have tortured her in the prison cell, if they had got the chance.

Finally, the boat shuffles towards the landing stage and the tourists raise their voices even louder as they pick out their preferred seats from the bank. Eva tries a little double bluff, darting in between the family groups, as though wishing to alight unnoticed. She is relieved to see, out of the corner of her eye, that they have taken the bait and are swaggering towards the boat as though they had been waiting for it all morning.

Her heart misses a small beat as she steps on to the craft, but she has no time for theatrics. She strides to the front of the boat and settles herself facing the lake. Its beauty, even now, threatens to smother her, almost as though it lacked discretion. She closes her eyes and listens for the roar of the engine and the swing of the bow towards Luino.

Once they are a few hundred metres away from Cannero, Eva risks a glance behind her to reassure herself that the guards got on the boat. She spots them towards the back of the boat. With a start, she notices a familiar igure sitting with them. Marco has joined them at their table. Her horror quickly turns to anger, her face smarting from the blow that he inflicted on her. Rather than prompting her fear that the same might happen again, his presence makes her more resolute. He can hit her all he wants, because, at this very minute, Stephen is escaping these callous men.

Again, she has to stop herself from laughing at the sight of the four of them bent across their table, mumbling in low voices, or pretending to look at the horizon, while they monitor her position. Then, shifting slightly, she feels the weight of the gun in the bag on her lap and is brought back to reality. She tries to gain some reassurance from the ice-topped mountains that rise up behind Luino.

By the time she reaches the main road on the lakefront of Luino, the quartet are hardly attempting to disguise the fact that they are following her. She can almost hear their breathing above the clatter of their footsteps behind her, as she quickens her pace along the street.

While the men pause to stare at a woman with Nordic features, she darts up a side street and then into a dark cafe, where a few old men are playing cards and smoking around some grubby tables. She moves close to the dingy counter and then sees Stella, the blonde woman from the shop, who is sipping an espresso next to her. She says nothing, but nods to the doorway behind the counter. A dusty sheet has been hung across it to stop the customers witnessing their efforts at cooking.

"Go straight through," she whispers. "The back door leads straight on to the park."

Eva nods her thanks and slips past the sheet. The

kitchen, disinfectant barely disguising the whiff of rotting food, is deserted. As she opens the door to the park, she hears the guards coming through the front door, but she is sure the customers will not betray her.

The park is small but it is thick with foliage. She is hurrying to the far gate when she hears the church bell strike two. The return ferry does not leave until five. Her work is done and she didn't even need the gun. Stephen will be free, armed with his new passport, heading across the hills towards Switzerland. She has three hours to kill before she can return. Suddenly, she remembers the art gallery whose address Amelia had scribbled down on her note. It must have some significance or why would Amelia have included it? She finds the note in her pocket and reads "Galleria Moderna, Via Giovanni Carnovali, Luino."

Dropping her jacket behind a bush and pulling her scarf close around her chin, Eva adopts an elderly stoop as she walks out of the park. An ancient resident gives her directions and within five minutes, she is on the Via Giovanni Carnovali. She soon finds the Galleria Moderna. Its windows are deep and long, illuminating a small gallery.

She pushes open the door and enters.

At first, it seems deserted. Then, she hears a small whimper from a door at the back of the room. A young woman appears carrying a baby on her hip. The baby, only a few months old, is in the initial stages of grizzling, its gentle whimper gradually taking on the music of conversation as the woman talks to it in soothing tones. When the two of them see Eva, they both grow quiet and an identical, cautious smile appears on their faces.

Eva smiles and greets them politely, then looks to the

wall. She sees greens, blues and whites, the signature of the area, that watery bliss so favoured by amateur painters, on the canvases around her. But these are not the idyllic scenes that most painters produce. These, in bold and broad brushstrokes, have the same threat that Eva sees all around her. In the triangles and circles, light and dark, lurks a menace that threatens to overwhelm the viewer. Eva is mesmerised.

"You like them, eh?" The young woman is approaching Eva, the baby still hooked on her hip.

"They are... perfect." She does not take her eyes from the canvases, her head spins as she tries to take them all in at once. "Who is the artist?" She leans in close to one of the paintings to scrutinise the signature. "This... Adelina Carmine? Is she a local artist?"

"That is me. I am the artist. Can I interest you in buying one of my works?"

"Me? Oh no. I am here just to... I mean, I represent a buyer in Milan. A gallery owner... on the Corso Matteotti." Eva's readiness to deceive surprises herself, but she quickly warms to her role, pulling herself up in height. "Yes, these are interesting... pieces. How long have you been painting? And where did you train?"

While she talks, the pictures begin to work a strange magic. The mountains, made of streaks of purple and cream begin to whisper to her of loneliness and abandonment. The isolation that she has felt since moving here is intensified. She is glad to hear Adelina's voice cutting through her reverie.

"... Of course, I don't paint any more, as I have other things to think about." Her face leans towards the top of the baby's head and she can't resist taking in his sweet smell as she inhales. "And, well, art is hardly an acceptable career in these times, when people have so little. Even the tourists sense our desperation and are eager to keep hold of their currencies."

"Yes, I suppose so," replies Eva. "When there is nothing to eat, art, I suppose, becomes a luxury and loses its meaning."

Eva follows Adelina's gaze to the windows. She is relieved to see that there are no uniforms in sight. Neither are there prospective customers.

"Well, I must close for lunch now, signorina. Matteo will be getting hungry." She gives the baby a squeeze and it chuckles in reply. Eva has never seen a happier baby. However, the guards could discover her at any time if she goes back out on to the street. She has to think quickly.

"I would love to see more of your work. You have a considerable talent."

"Thank you…"

"Call me Eva."

Eva takes the young woman's outstretched hand and, for the first time, sees the sadness hidden in the corners of her mouth.

"Would you be able to come to my home, Eva? I have many examples of my work there. Nothing recent, of course… but I still like some of it."

"Certainly, Adelina. I would love to." Eva feels the shaky satisfaction of her own desire coinciding with circumstance, for the second time today.

Together, they close up the shop. Adelina hands the baby to Eva while she locks the front door. Side by side, they walk up through the town towards the mountains, after ten minutes, they are at the gate of a small farmstead, consisting of a two-storey farmhouse, a couple of dilapidated outbuildings and a few ramshackle pens, one of which is occupied by a large, elderly-looking pig.

"My family were farmers once, but now there is only my father and I, so we cannot..."

"Matteo's father, then, is he... not living here?"

Adelina's head drops. Her sigh is smothered in the baby's head.

"No, he is not here. He is... gone. We were to be married, but my father did not wish..." Her eyes fill with an emotion that is more resentment than sorrow.

Eva places her hand gently on Adelina's forearm. "I am sorry," she says. "I should not have asked."

Adelina's eyes start to fill with tears. "Come, let us go inside."

They go into a darkened room warmed by a stove. Around the walls lean various spades and forks. Together, they sit at a gnarled table, where Adelina starts to nurse Matteo, who gurgles contentedly.

"How old is Matteo?" Eva asks.

"He is three months. But he is already smiling... you see?" Another wide grin from the baby and Eva feels herself falling a little in love with him.

While he nurses, he emits a low hum that Adelina sings back to him. Eva draws her eyes from the tableau they form and looks out of the window, that gives on to the path they just walked up. Surely nobody would look for her here? And yet an uneasiness, linked to the task of diverting the attention of the guards, is making her heart race.

"He looks like his father," says Adelina, not taking her eyes from her son. Something about the sadness in her voice, and the glint of chestnut around the crown of baby hair, makes Eva look up at her with a start. Of course, she thinks, this is Sam's baby. If Sam had been in Luino for a year, he would have had time to meet this woman and have a baby with her.

"Adelina!" Her mind is racing. What does this woman know about the death of her baby's father? Doe she even know that he is dead. She said that he is 'gone' but she sounded more deserted than bereaved. "Adelina," she repeats more softly, "tell me about him... if you want to. If it would help... I mean."

Adelina looks towards the window, far away, through its grimy smears and out towards the Swiss mountains it frames. "He is a gentle man. Funny, always making jokes to lighten the burden of life. But serious... you know... when it is necessary."

"Is he from around here?" Eva keeps her excitement from her voice. Could she be about to solve the mystery that has occupied her thoughts since that night in the church, and changed everything for her?

Adelina's eyes moisten again. "No. If only he had been a local boy, but... you know what these boys are like, yes? There are only the fascists left here."

"I could not be happy with someone like that, either."

Eva waits, Adelina clearly wants to talk. She has not told this story and it is corroding inside her. Her longing to speak just the name of her lover is so strong that Eva has only to wait patiently. Besides, she calculates, if she is wrong, it will be easier for her to walk away without an explanation if she has simply let Adelina tell her tale at her own pace.

"Sam is English. He came here with his work over a year ago." Adelina turns her gaze back to her child, who is still suckling and humming. "We were to be married. But… I knew he was Jewish so I kept it to myself. My father, he… well, when he found out, he didn't approve. He sent Sam away. He said it would be better if the child were fatherless than… I began to see his point of view. It was… a mistake. Life is not like in the movies. I did not feel so strongly for Sam that I wanted to leave my home. But now we are on our own and I am lonely and I sometimes wonder…"

She trails off and the tears anoint her baby's head. He stops humming and stares up at his mother.

"I am sorry, Adelina, so sorry."

Adelina turns to Eva with a quizzical look. "Why should you be sorry? It was a mistake and he has gone back to England… And I have Matteo to love now."

Eva looks deep into Adelina's face.

So this is the moment I finally grow up, thinks Eva.

"Adelina, I am sorry to tell you this——"

She is interrupted by the sound of footsteps. Adelina is already on her feet, staring down the path. Eva turns to see a tall man in uniform approaching and it takes an instant to recognise Severino, the senior guard who has been following her.

She looks at Adelina, who sees her desperation.

"Don't worry, Eva, You have nothing to fear from my father."

"No, you don't understand! That man… is your father?" She cannot keep the terror from her voice.

She turns her head away at the moment that Severine spots her. Her position, sitting submissively at the table immediately feels pathetic. How could she have made such a mistake as to come here? But it is too late to move away. And now, the person who surely must have murdered Sam is approaching her, with a look of unchecked fury on his face. And something else. A recognition of opportunity.

CHAPTER 17

"Adelina. Quick, I need to tell you something—"

But it is too late. Severino has reached the door at a run. He hurls it open. Eva registers the effort he has made to frighten her. It has not come naturally to him.

"You!" he spits with his voice as he strides towards the table. "What are you doing here? What are you telling my daughter?"

Eva shrinks towards the back wall. Then, remembering the gun in her bag, she stops herself and holds her ground.

"What have you to hide, signore? What should you have told your daughter — and, more importantly, your grandson — about his father?"

For a moment, he is lost for words. But the spittle glowing on his chin shows his feeling. "What are you talking about? What has Matteo got to do with you?"

Eva's mind races. Severino does not have the wit, in her quickened estimation, to act the innocent. If Severino cannot make the connection between her and Sam, then he does not know of the existence of Stephen, or that

Stephen identified the body that was pulled out of the lake. And why would he? Everybody else, including his own daughter, thinks that Sam was simply persuaded to go back to England. Could Severino forgive himself for murdering a Jewish man who seduced his daughter and so nearly brought shame on to the family?

"How can you say that? Taking a man's life means so little to you? You are worse than... than... the Germans!"

Adelina turns away from the cot, where she has been hurriedly stowing the baby, who is already growing agitated at the raised voices and temperatures, to stare at her father.

"What does she mean, Papa? What man's life has been taken?" Her voice is steady but contains a sharp thread of panic that is ready to slice her composure.

"She is talking nonsense!" His hardening face shows that a rising rage is his only option in the face of two frantic young women. "This woman is wanted by the police in Cannero." His breathing slows slightly. "I have orders to take her back there right now." He makes a move towards Eva but she ducks around the table behind Adelina, who instinctively moves away from both of them to return to the cradle. She places her back against it and spreads her arms to each corner, her chin raised.

"One of you has to tell me what is going on... and what this woman has to do with Sam!"

Eva also spreads her palms. "I never knew him, Adelina, I swear." Only her fear stops her from crying. "I swear I only saw Sam once. And even then I had no idea of his name. But, oh Adelina, he was dead!"

"Dead? No, he can't be! He is back in England. I am

expecting a letter from him."

"I am so sorry, Adelina. I had to attend to his wake at the church in Cannero. Nobody knew him, except for one other man, and he did not dare speak his name."

"But it can't be Sam. How... how can you know it was him?"

"I worked it out from... But there is no time to explain. Just ask your father if I speak the truth."

Severino looks from one face to the other, unable to speak. His open mouth suspends his breathing for a long minute, then, slowly, he sinks to the chair and holds his head in his hands.

Suddenly, Eva forgets the feelings of everyone else in the room. The shock of Adelina, the bitter remorse of her father. Instead, she is filled with rage at all the lies she has faced in the last few days. And before that, the anger at having to move to Cannero from Milan, the acid strain of keeping her mother in a good mood, of never understanding who her mother was... and the terrible grief of never having known her father.

"Admit it, you brute!" she screams. "You killed him and threw him in the lake. You left him to rot in there while you carried on persecuting innocent people. And all because he had different beliefs to you? What kind of warped and dangerous mind do you have? How can you let him near your baby, Adelina? He needs to be locked up... for murder!"

The baby is crying now, but Adelina's whisper cuts through the noise. "Is this true, Papa?"

Severino's tears become plentiful. "My own daughter... how can you know the troubles that are coming? You do not see what I see — the threat from the other side, over there." His chin juts out towards the mountains where Germany waits to pounce. "I see and hear terrible things when I am on my patrols."

"But how—?" Adelina interrupts.

"No, wait!" He bangs his hand on the table. "I admit it. I admit that I did not want you to marry the Jewish boy. Having a Jewish husband can only bring you trouble, I know. The stories I hear. Just last week, there was a couple murdered in Austria for having those beliefs. I could not watch you put yourself in danger. And you seemed so happy with the baby. I thought... I thought he would be enough for you."

"So you killed him?" Adelina's hands go to her mouth, her fists crammed against her teeth.

"No! Adeline, believe me! I arranged to meet him last week. I told him to leave. He said that, even if he went now, he would be back to collect you and Matteo. I got angry. I roughed him up a little and I told him that even if he could convince you to go to England, he would never see Matteo again. That I would never let my grandson leave Italy and grow up... a Jew. But I never killed him. When I left him, he was alive."

"So Eva must have got it wrong. It must have been somebody else in the church. People drown all the time. Why couldn't it have been a tourist?"

"Yes, it must have been, my dear." He stands and turns again to Eva. "What gives you the right to come in here and accuse me of such terrible things? Trying to blame me for the death of a drunk tourist? What on earth gave you the idea it was Sam?"

Eva sobs. "I don't know! I found out little by little. There was nothing to identify him at the time. They all thought it was a nobody, a stranger, as though a stranger didn't matter. But I couldn't bring myself to feel that way. I wanted to know who it was, so I searched him. All I found on the body was half a ticket."

"A ticket?" Adelina looks up.

"Yes, a ferry ticket for Luino. Used. Ripped in half. It was sewn into his jacket. It was what made me come over the lake in the first—"

"Where?"

"What? To Luino. I came here a few days—"

"No! Where on his jacket? Where was the ticket sewn?"

Eva's eyes open wide. "It was behind the left lapel. Deep into the seam. I would never have found it but I—"

Adelina sinks to the floor. Her father runs to her side, picks her up and pushes her down on to a chair, where she lays on the table, limp. After a few seconds, she seems to come to herself again. She looks around, remembers where she is. Then she spots Eva and the truth hits her again.

"It was him," she says with a deathly composure. "He wanted to keep that ticket to remind him of the night we... the night we made Matteo. He made me sew it into his lapel. Over his heart." She draws her arms round her lowered head and holds herself and her memories of him tight and still, while the baby's cries soften to nothing. In a tiny whisper, she starts to speak, repeating the same words louder and louder, until Eva can hear their shape. "He was telling the truth. He was telling the truth. He was telling the truth!"

Adelina's head raises and she waits a few seconds to regain the strength in order to continue.

"He told me," she sobs. "He told me, when he found out that I was pregnant, that, to him, a baby was not just a plaything, an annoyance, or a millstone, or any of those things that we think men will see them as. To him, a baby was a solemn responsibility, a commitment to the future that gave him not only joy, but something else. A meaning. He said that it was his belief that one of the duties of being a father was teaching a child how to swim. When I laughed at him, he explained that it meant more than just swimming, it meant teaching a child how to stay afloat, no matter what life threw at them. I told him that he should wait until it started keeping him up at nights. But I saw that he was becoming angry when I laughed. He said that if I ever stopped him from being a father to the baby he would not know what to do. That it might, it might… send him so crazy that he would not know how to live. I wanted to laugh again — he was being so dramatic — but I stopped myself and we soon went back to normal and I forgot all about it. But now I see how it happened." She turns to her father, "Papa, when you told him that he would never see Matteo again, it overwhelmed him. He couldn't go on, so he…"

Silence wreathes the room. Eva weighs up the evidence like a judge, in the midst of the grief. Either Severino is lying and his pride in the purity of his family line led him to murder, or he delivered the final blow, by forbidding Sam to see his son. She knows that, in the eyes of the law, the former is a mortal sin, while the latter, well, it attaches no guilt at all to Severino's actions. But this does not tell the whole story. She regrets her lack of worldly experience hat would allow her to make sense of this. Would a man be able to commit suicide over such a thing as not being able to see his baby? She has never considered the possibility. She thinks again of her father. Would he have felt like that about her? She will never know.

Severino stumbles over to his daughter, who has gathered Matteo in her arms. He accompanies her out of the room and Eva hears noises of his comforting her and helping her to lie down. His voice is gentle and soothing and Eva is so astonished at its tenderness that she doesn't think of escaping until he stops talking. The scrape of his chair in the next room brings her to her senses and she makes a rush for the front door.

But it is locked. She did not notice Severino locking it. She rattles the door, in case it is simply stuck, but it will not budge.

"Leave it, signorina." His voice has the calmness of an assassin.

"You cannot keep me here," Eva cries. "I have done nothing wrong."

"That's not what they are saying at the station, signorina. They are saying that you are involved in a plot to assassinate Mussolini. That you would have done the deed at Borromeo if you hadn't been stopped. That you would be hanging on a gibbet right now if you hadn't bribed an official to release you from the cell at the palace. Or seduced him, some say."

Sensing the move his remarks are making, Eva reaches into her bag and her hand closes around the cold weight of the gun. In a second, she has pulled it out and pointed it at Severino.

"Open the door. You have no right to keep me here. Unlock it. Now!"

She cocks the gun, just like she has seen in the movies. Her hands are barely shaking, as though she was born for a gunfight.

Severino shuffles towards a cabinet and takes a rusty old key from a hook behind it. Eva moves around behind the table, allowing him a clear passage towards the door. He reaches it and unlocks it. All this time, he has barely looked at Eva. He holds the door open and gestures for her to exit by passing right next to him. But she waggles her gun at him and he retreats into the room and tucks himself behind the table, across from Eva, who edges through the door looking backwards towards him.

Then she is running down the muddy path, her gun useless in her hands.

Only then does she consider that Severino might have a gun in the house. He was not wearing one on his belt when he came in, she is sure, but he could fetch one in seconds.

She drops behind the pig pen — only a number of dilapidated greening planks making their way back to the earth — and waits, breathing heavily. After a long minute, she pokes her head up to glance back at the house. Nothing is moving.

But then she sees a flash of metal and Severino's hand is poking from behind the door jamb. A shot rings out as she sinks back to the ground.

Then suddenly, impossibly, Marco is there. His shot is aimed high — a warning only. He throws his body beside hers and looks at her as though she is a strange bedfellow.

Her first instinct is to run. Then she turns her gun on him.

"Get back! Get away from me!"

"Eva, you have it all wrong. I want——"

"I know what you want, you bastard. The same as at Borromeo. To lock me up and throw away the key."

"You are wrong, Eva," Marco is breathing hard. "I saved you at Borromeo."

Eva drops her gun to the ground, glad to relinquish its ugly weight. Marco makes no move to grab it. Eva stares at him. "What on earth do you mean?" The memory of his hand hitting her face wields its own logic, that cannot be shifted in her mind.

"I'm sorry I hit you, Eva. I had to make it look good and it was all I could think of."

She searches his face for any sign of duplicity but finds only sorrow drawing its stripe between his brows.

"You were in great danger at the Palace, Eva." Marco takes a look over the top of the pig pen but there is no sign of Severino. "There had already been one woman assaulted that morning in Il Duce's rooms. I could not let that happen to you."

"Assaulted? What do you mean?" And then it comes back to her. The girl running into the kitchen, her clothes askew, her tears all used up.

"I never believed what people had been saying about Mussolini," Marco sighs. "About his... appetites. The women, the girls. People say all sorts of things to disparage the powerful. But I could not let you enter that room. I couldn't. And now... now, I can't be a soldier any more, either. I can't be part of this regime. I am going overseas."

Eva cannot speak. The reality of the danger she had been in at Borromeo, combined with the realisation that the person she has hated the most, throughout this ordeal, was the one who saved her, cannot be put into words.

Instead, she whispers, "Marco…" as the sound of a footstep and the click of a gun being cocked alert them to the approach of Severino.

"Put down the gun, officer."

Without looking up, Marco places his gun on the ground in front of him.

"Now, both of you stand up."

Eva looks from Severino to Marco, who nods and they both shuffle to their feet, their hands outstretched like they were giving a blessing. Severino lifts the gun to their chest height.

Marco steps in front of Eva.

"Let her go, Severino." Marco's voice is steady. "She has done nothing wrong."

"Hah!" Severino laughs. "What has she promised you now, officer, eh? A couple of days ago, she was enemy number one, according to you!"

"It was all a stupid mistake. She is no more harm than… than this rotten pigsty."

Severino does not hesitate. "You can explain what you like to the Commissario once I have you both locked up. Now, walk!"

As Severino indicates the front gate with the tip of his gun, Marco lunges forward. Their bodies collide and their arms scramble for supremacy. Severino's gun lifts higher and Marco tries to squeeze it from his grasp.

"Run!" he shouts.

Eva darts along the path and through the front gate. It
is not until she is back on the street that she hears a shot.
She has left her gun in the mud between their feet.

CHAPTER 18

She has no idea how long she hides in the forest on the outskirts of the town. It lines the road leading to Switzerland and is largely ignored by tourists, who are drawn to the water, its oily glints so mesmerising that to turn back to the woodland seems an insult to its beauty.

Running to the darkness of its foliage seemed a natural move after she ran from Adelina's house. The road outside the farmhouse twisted up towards its heights and Eva knew that going back down to the town, where more guards may be waiting for her, made no sense.

At first, her senses are too acute to allow her to think clearly. When she hears footsteps, she withdraws further into the forest, thankful that her clothes are dark and unlikely to stand out. But it is only boys collecting firewood or ancient, mushroom-seeking men. There is no sign of the guards.

The sound of the gunshot has focused all her attention on her own safety. She knows she must not be found. All suspicion for whatever has happened at Adelina's will naturally fall on her. The guards will be scouring the town looking for her.

She tries to make sense of what happened back at Adelina's house. The gunshot. What could it mean? Has Severino been shot? Or Marco? Her anxiety allows her only to think of what these scenarios might mean for her own safety.

The woodland interruptions become less frequent as night falls. The sounds of the town have faded to near silence, the birds have settled and the nocturnal animals are starting to stir when she finally emerges on to the street. A mist clings to the buildings, rendering the town almost obscure. Eva picks her way down the narrow street to the town. Here, the light from the some of the hotels casts a faint glow on to the road. Eva moves away from the windows where the guests are clinking glasses over their evening meals.

She has to get back to Cannero, to speak to her mother and to find Padre Giacomo, in order to decide what to do next. Maybe they can smuggle her out of the country, like they did Stephen. She walks to the edge of the lake, a little south of the jetty, and looks across. Cannero, on the other side, must be over a mile away. The ferries stopped running at sundown, but she would not have risked such a journey, anyway, with the guards on the lookout for her.

Swimming is out of the question.

There is only one option left to her.

She walks further south, away from the Swiss border, towards the little homesteads that border the lake before the forest engulfs the shoreline. A slither of beach is illuminated by the moon. At last she finds what she is looking for. A rowing boat nestled in the scrub at the top of the beach. The wooden craft is a few feet wide and, when Eva gives it a shake, it seems sturdily constructed.

She stows her bag deep in its bow.

She pulls the boat by the rope at its prow from the top of the beach down the few short feet towards the water. It scrapes along the screed with an excited outbreath and glides into the water. As she has seen the fishermen do, she throws the rope into the boat and places one foot into it, feeling her weight upset its balance. Then, almost by instinct, she holds on to the opposite side with her hand and presses down hard, allowing the rest of her body enough space to slip into the hull of the boat. She sits on the thin slat of wood for a few seconds, feeling the little waves that lap the beach lift and drop her. She holds her breath as she lifts the oars, one at a time, from the floor to the crutches that have been fixed to each side of her. All the time, the silence around her is oppressive, and every little sound the boat makes echoes around the lake like an ill-kept rumour.

She lays both the oars flat on the water. The water holds them up as firmly as if it were liquid concrete, allowing her to move around a little bit, to twist her head in order to see where she is going. She has noticed how the fishermen head out to the open water with their bodies backwards, facing away from their goal. It takes her a moment to orientate herself, but she is glad to see that there is only one set of twinkling lights on the opposite shore that mark her destination. The currents have twisted the boat so that she is already facing away from it, and she figures that her boat will go the right way, if only she can get the oars up and away from their resting place in the leaden, tugging water and put them into action.

She lifts the oars by pressing her hands to her knees. Immediately, the boat starts to wobble. With a gasp, she sets the oars back on to the water, flat, and waits for the rocking to subside.

She tries again. This time, she raises the oars just a few inches. There is still a tremor but the rocking is less severe.

She does this lifting motion a few times, observing how the wobbling is reduced if she holds her body rigid at its centre. Then, she adds a twist in her wrists until the oars are perpendicular to the water.

She waits a few moments and then finally, she pushes the oars a little behind her, sets the points into the water and pulls with all her might. Movement! The oars seem to lift themselves out of the water at the other end of the stroke and she hovers for a moment, scarcely believing that it is so easy. She takes another couple of strokes: short, choppy jabs that do not result in any progress but keep the boat balanced at least. Then another long stroke.

She starts to relax.

She plans a long stroke and pushes the oars behind her even further. But something goes wrong with the right oar. Instead of gliding through the water horizontally, something drags at it from beneath the surface, dragging it down. She tries to pull it back with all her strength but, whatever is holding it pulls harder, forcing the right side of the boat down until Eva can see the water start to inch over it. She lets go of the oar and immediately the boat rights itself, but the oar has been pulling her so hard that when she releases it she is thrown off balance, hurling her backwards. She hits her head on the rudder as she lands on the bottom of the boat.

She lies on the cold, damp wood long enough to forget where she is when she comes round. Her eyes open to the darkness with only the lapping sound reminding her of where she is. She sits up slowly, being careful not to rock the boat. Eventually, she is able to slither back on the wooden slat by slipping her legs over it and pushing with her hands. She reaches out her hands. She can only find one oar, which she must have pulled into the boat when she fell backwards. The other one must be in the lake.

She looks around, orienting herself. While she was dazed in the bottom of the boat, she has drifted further from the shore, which she can just make out in the gloom.

She turns and fixes the twinkling of Cannero in her sights. Instinctively, she rows with a new strength as two hands grip tight, digging the remaining oar into the water and scooping it past her. When she moves a few inches, she switches the oar to the other side in order to straighten up. She makes some awkward progress like this. Her arms are already starting to ache when the oar bangs against something.

She looks down. Her mind is filled with images of bones or bodies, but it is the oar that she lost a few minutes ago, caught up in the same swirl and, miraculously, following her route. Tentatively, she reaches down and plucks it from the water, ignoring the rocking motion her action produces.

She fits both oars into their cradles and then uses just her right hand to turn the boat through a half circle, until

ıe is facing away from Cannero again, and points her
ars behind her for her first stroke.

Always a practical girl.

Her father's voice echoes across like a soft mist. A
ıemory floods over her. A trip in a boat with her father.
riendly water splashing around them.

But how could that be? She could scarcely walk before
ıe went off to war. She must be losing her mind.

But his words reassure her.

She has held on to the oars for a full ten strokes now.
)n the eleventh, she feels the same tug dragging her right
ıar out of her hand again, but she is swift enough to pull
t out of the water before it becomes engulfed again. This
ʒives her the confidence to increase the power behind
:ach stroke, until she feels she is travelling a few metres
vith each one.

When she looks over her shoulder, the ruined castle
ɔn Cannero Island is coming into view out of the dark,
ı dim shadow rearing up out of the shimmering water,
naybe half a mile away, or one hundred metres. She has
ıo idea. Another few minutes, the slow ache that started
ın her neck and threatened to envelop her whole body,
ʌarms to nothing as her body heats up. She has achieved
ı rhythm now: a pull through the resisting waves, a beat, a
slow return of the oars through the air.

Yes, I am a practical girl, she thinks.

Being on the lake makes her feel safe. No one can
reach her. In the gloom and with only the gentle splash
of the oars to accompany her thoughts, the events of the
afternoon take over again.

First, the gunshot. The fact that nobody came to look

for her in the forest makes her think that Severino must have been killed or wounded by Marco in the struggle. That must be it. Marco would have taken him inside and he and Adelina would have cared for him if the injury was not too bad. Or if it had been serious, they would have called for help. Either way, Marco must have explained to them that she was innocent of everything of which she is accused.

But then she remembers fragments of what Marco first said.

He said he had saved her from Mussolini at the Borromeo palace.

Was she really in danger? And from Mussolini himself?

The idea seems preposterous. But…

She pictures the girl in the green dress at the palace running through the kitchen, her tears dripping from her chin. These terrible images echo around the boat as it makes its gentle progress towards Cannero. If he is telling the truth then she owes him everything.

Then her horror fixes itself on Adelina, Matteo and poor Sam, drowned in this very lake that is taking her home. Can she believe Severino? He said that he had warned Sam that he would never see Matteo again if he stayed in Italy. But he denied killing him. And Adelina's chilling words: that Sam wanted to teach his child how to swim, to teach him how to stay afloat, no matter what life threw at him. Could being prevented from doing so have forced him to commit suicide?

Suddenly she remembers her first conversation with Stephen at the wake. That must be what he had meant when he asked Eva to investigate Sam's death. For some reason, he wanted her to understand that men too can love a child to distraction, that men can turn the loss of their child on themselves, can allow it to destroy them to the point of making life not worth living. In fact, those had been Stephen's words: "I just want to bring this man's story into the light." He thought nobody would listen to a man, so he had asked Eva to find out what had happened, just as nobody believed that Sam could care so much for his own child that he would take his own life when he was denied access to him.

Finally, Eva finds herself pressing her boat into the little beach, just as the first rays of the sun peak through the wooded valleys behind the town, breathing life onto the blue grey sand.

CHAPTER 19

Eva can hear the hum of voices, as she approaches the archway that leads round the corner to her street. There is enough light to see the crowd of guards assembled around the front gate of the house.

The last few hours have taught her to not be surprised at anything. Eva now knows her mother well enough to be sure that she would not allow herself to be trapped by such blunt instruments as these men.

She silently retreats and walks back along the lake path. She resolves that, if anyone approaches her from the other direction, she will jump into the water and hide beneath the bank.

She smiles.

Yesterday, that would have been unthinkable.

It is too early for tourists. The hotel workers will arrive soon. Only the birdsong begins to disturb the silence as she passes the factory, standing sentinel over the still grey water.

Eva begins the slow climb up the hill towards the San Giorgio church. It has been less than a week since she first set eyes on Sam, but now she thinks she understands what happened and why. Yes, she has been naive, impetuous and stupid. She has been brought closer to death than she realised at the time. But, now, there is only one person who needs to unpick the final threads.

Paola.

By the time she reaches the stepping-stones that lead up the hill towards the church, the sun has started to illuminate the top of the spire. She quickens her pace. The day is nearly breaking, meaning churchgoers arriving, eager for morning prayers.

She can smell the smoke of the candles as she enters the building, where the son of Giacomo's housekeeper must have just fulfilled his morning duty of extinguishing them. A little too early, as there is hardly any light penetrating the windows yet.

She shakes off her giddiness and calls out, "Giacomo!" She could wonder where she found such boldness — to shout in a church. She knows, although she could not explain how, it came from the water. From overcoming her dislike of it, yes, but something else, too.

"Giacomo!" she shouts again, the echoes returning to her from behind the saints' effigies.

The curtain of the confessional shifts and Giacomo emerges.

"I have been waiting for you, Eva!" His cassock is still heavily stained, but he walks with dignity, the affected drunkenness shaken off. "Quickly!" he whispers, "Your mother is waiting for you in my apartments."

He strides away from her, towards the door set back from the front pews. He looks back over his shoulder and beckons to her immobile figure. "Come, come! We can't wait a moment longer. You have heard about Marco, I suppose? Such a shame. He could have been useful."

"Wait!" she runs after his retreating figure, her sandals tapping irreverently against the flagstones. "Marco is dead? But… but how have you heard? I was there. I saw him last night."

"We know that, Eva," he says, over his shoulder. "That brute Severino is putting it about that you killed Marco, but we knew that was hardly likely. Still, you have turned up the heat over here. Guards everywhere. We have had to make other plans for the two of you."

"The two of…?" But Giacomo has disappeared into his apartment. She runs to catch up before the heavy door bangs in her face.

From the hallway, Eva spots Paola standing at Giacomo's kitchen table, packing a small suitcase. Looking up, Paola gasps and runs to her daughter.

"Where are you going?" Eva puts up her hands to stop her mother barging into her.

"My darling Eva! Thank God! There was no mention of you when the word came through about Marco, so we had reason to hope, but I am so glad to see you in the flesh."

"Where are you going?" she repeats.

"What, this?" She looks back at the suitcase, then rushes back to her work of stuffing clothing into it. "Yes, our plans have changed since we got word of what happened in Luino. But don't worry, we know it's not your fault.

Luckily I keep some things here for just such an occasion as this." She picks up a stocking from the floor and holds it out to Eva. "Can you help? Our mountain guide comes in an hour. He will accompany us to our hiding place on Cannero island until nightfall when we can set off."

"Set off?" Eva stands rigid in the doorway. She can hear Giacomo in the room behind her, opening and shutting drawers. "Where?"

Finally Paola stops folding and looks up at Eva. "Across the border. We are going to Switzerland, of course, where we can catch a train to Paris tomorrow morning."

"We?" Eva voice starts to rise in horror. "I'm not going anywhere with you! You sent me as bait to Borromeo when you must have known that I was just a titbit to be devoured by that pig."

Paola sits down at the kitchen table slowly.

"Come. Let me explain." Her voice is soft but Eva detects an equality in it, something more than the gentleness of a mother explaining the facts of life to her too-innocent child. Otherwise, Eva tells herself, I would walk out of this room and this town.

She lowers herself into one of Giacomo's chairs smoothed sleek with use.

Paola begins.

"We haven't much time, Eva. But the facts are these: while everyone was at the conference, I managed to help two Jewish families get out of Italy. The conference took up everybody's time; they were all turning the other way. It was a gift."

"But you let me go there. Your own daughter! To provide a decoy."

"I love Mussolini no more than you do, Eva. He is a tyrant and a brute, I agree. But it is too easy to believe everything you hear about him. Such as he eats live animals. Or he has to have three different women a day. We play into his hands by building up this picture of him. A superhuman, even a bad one, is more able to control people. And by believing these stories, we divert our attention from the less exciting work of providing an alternative."

"But Marco believed them because... because he saw what Mussolini did to that girl and he knew that I was next."

"That may be. In which case he did you a great favour. But we will never know what really happened to that girl. The same as we will never really know what would have happened to you in Mussolini's room if you had entered it. You may have made a good sale!"

Eva looks at Paola as though she is seeing her for the first time. Marco risked his life for her at Borromeo, and now he is dead. And her mother is making jokes.

"You are... you really are... despicable."

"Eva, Eva!" Paola's voice thickens. "When a man is powerful, it is easy to believe bad stories about him. Think about what you saw, Eva. A girl crying. Did you see him attack her? No, but you say Marco did. But all he really saw was a girl running from Il Duce's room and he, quite naturally, came to a simple conclusion. And of course we cannot ask him now. But think about it. How do we know that Il Duce was not reprimanding her for stealing, or treason, or an attempt on his life? Well, we will never know now. Marco is dead and we are all in danger. So we must leave."

Eva does not move. She wants to cry but somehow this unveiling of her mother, colder and more heartless than the fascist she was imitating for so many years, requires a different reaction.

"I am glad," Eva says, at last, "that my father never saw this."

"Saw what, exactly, Eva?" Paola's gaze tightens. "A woman defending what she believes in? Yes, I suppose he would have found that difficult to witness. Considering…"

Eva's head twitches imperceptibly. "Considering what?"

"Look, Eva." Paola bangs her hand on the table in a quiet rhythm. "Your father. Well, his principles were more easily forgotten, shall we say."

"What are you talking about?" Eva's voice rises. "He died for his country! How much more principled did he have to be to please you?"

Paola gets up and walks to the window where a fly is trying to escape. She sighs.

"It is all the same thing, Eva." The fly's buzzing moves up a tone. "There is no such thing as a hero. Your father's actions at Caporetto… well, for years I could hardly bear to think about them without anger."

"Caporetto?" Eva interrupts, pulling her mother's shoulder around to face her. "He was there? Where the soldiers were dying of cold and starvation? Where they were so desperate that they mutinied? Why didn't you tell me?"

"The shame of it was overwhelming, Eva. I told no one when I found out that he had deserted. The things people were saying about the men — it was unbearable to think that he—. I took you and left my home, my family and everything I knew. That's when we went to Milan where nobody knew us."

"But my father was in Milan! I remember him. I remember him calling me his Scintilla and rowing with me in the canal before the war!"

"No, Eva. That was in my hometown. It was… somewhere else miles from Milan." Paola closes the suitcase. "We started a new life. It was hard, God knows, but in Milan we could live without the shame of what he had done."

"What he had done!" Eva is shaking. "You mean he tried to escape?" Her mother's silence allows the logic of her words to fall into place. "But wait a minute. How would you know that he tried to escape? Unless he…"

Paola sinks back to her chair. "I couldn't let you grow up with a man like that. Just knowing that he… gave up… I couldn't bear it. I couldn't allow it."

"But… You mean he is still alive?"

At last, Paola looks directly at Eva. Her eyes are alive with regret and longing but her words are urgent.

"If you are coming with me to Paris, Eva, we need to leave now."

Paris. There was a time, just a few days ago, when the prospect of visiting such a city would have been everything Eva had dreamed of. The glamour, the starlets, the clothes and the promise of some freedom. But everything has now changed. In the last few minutes. In the last few days. Eva can hardly look at her mother.

Paola purses her lips and starts to rummage in her bag.

Eventually, she pulls out a crumpled, yellowing envelope.

"Fine. If you are not coming, you will want to read this…"

Paola slams the envelope on the table. "And you had better hurry," she continues, "because it is Saturday today and you don't have much time."

Without turning to look back at Eva, Paola picks up her suitcase and walks back through the apartment and out into the church.

CHAPTER 20

Eva pulls her head back from the train window and sits down in her carriage. Giacomo's man has thrust a thousand-Lira note into her hand as the train pulled away from Stresa station, which she still crushes tightly in her fist. She shoves it into her pocket, then swipes the thick layer of dust from her skirts. Lying under sacks of grain on the back of the cart that brought her to the station has left her stiff and bruised, but she cannot complain.

Giacomo has worked a miracle to get her here.

From the window, she can see the carabinieri still gathered at the station entrance. They are searching the crowds of tourists for an Italian woman.

They are not looking for an old one, however. A few minutes ago, Eva was hobbling past them, pulling the dowager's headscarf donated by Giacomo closer to her chin. At just that moment, a noisy, red motorbike had cruised past the station, and the guards had all turned to follow its course towards the far corner, narrowing their yes in envy, while Eva had slipped on to the train.

Eva is now sitting in a carriage with just one other passenger, an elderly woman dozing in the corner. Eva tows her headscarf in her bag. As she presses her hand to the bottom of the bag, she realises that she will probably never see any of her treasured make-up again. But this eels more like shedding a skin than a sorrow.

She takes out the letter that Paola gave her. She has already read the first few lines back at the church. That was all it took to make up her mind to leave. She had run straight to Giacomo to tell him that she had to get to Milan as quickly as possible.

Now she starts reading again from the beginning:

24th November 1933

La mia piccola scintilla, My own little spark,

I have found you at last!

And you were not easy to find… Your mother has kept you well-hidden in Milan. It was only by the slimmest of chances that I met an English musician, who happened to mention a seamstress and her daughter who lived in his apartment block. And this was only because one of the buttons on my coat was missing. Imagine!

Just in case your mother is still too angry (and she was livid the last time we met), I hope this letter will let you find your own way to see me, if you want to. On Saturday at 5pm, I will wait on the bench at the foot of the statue of Vittorio Emanuele II. You know where it is outside the Duomo cathedral. I will wait for half an hour. You will know me by my blue handkerchief in my top pocket. I hope you will come. If you don't, I will be there the following Saturday at the same time, and I will keep going there until, one day, I hope you will come.

But, firstly, let me explain something.

People think that when two people fall in love, it is right to celebrate. And so they should, because when you meet the right boy or girl, it feels like you have won the lottery. And to marry, what greater achievement could there be? Family, friends, the whole world say, "Well done!"

But these congratulations are like a parent applauding a baby's first steps. That baby is doing those steps for himself. His smile might say otherwise but the instinct to move, to take a risk in order to evolve, is a selfish one. If he doesn't take that step, he will face all sorts of hardship. A human, even a tiny one, knows that without being told. It is the same for a new couple: their love is just nature's trick.

What I am saying is that anyone can fall in love. Our future depends on it.

I believe that the real cause for celebration should be when a couple faces their first test. When one of them says no and the other wants yes, now that is a proper test of true love. If they find a way to work together, that is when we should throw a party!

When I came back from the war, I had done something unforgivable, or so your mother thought. She said that by abandoning the army, I had brought shame on her family. She wanted nothing to do with me. I tried to change her mind but, by now, you must know what she is like! Nobody has ever changed her mind on anything.

But, what I need to tell you, dear Eva, is that I had a

duty to find those words that would have made her change her mind. Because of you.

Of course, I could not make her love me again. She is entitled to hate me for as long as she likes. But I should have found a way to convince her that you needed a father, no matter how pathetic a father she thought I was.

I should have found the right words. Or found somebody who knew them, and who could say them in the right way so that I could be a part of your life.

For your sake.

I am so sorry that I didn't.

Don't be angry at your mother for what she did. Protecting a child is the most natural thing in the world. But something being easy or natural is not enough. For instance, playing detective has come easily to me. It has taken me all these years, but I had natural patience and perseverance and now I have found your address. Others may call me a nuisance, an obsessive. You might think so, too.

But finding out where your mother ran to when she left our home town is pointless, if, like last time, I can't find the right words to make everything right.

When I got back from the war and your mother wanted to take you away from me, I didn't have the right words to stop her. And maybe no man ever has. If you meet me this weekend, or the next, or in a few years' time, I will not try to explain my failings — you know them all too well, my absence speaks of them to you every day — or attempt to justify myself. But I hope we can start to get to know each other, and become friends, in time.

With affection and love from your father.

§

Eva folds the letter back into its envelope and takes from her bag the embroidery she has been working on. It is only a few days since she abandoned it, but the work, a mountain and lake scene designed specifically for the tourist trade, appears from a different life. She selects a silver-grey thread and starts to sew.

"That is beautiful craftwork." The woman in the corner has woken up and leans towards Eva. "May I see it more closely?"

Eva stows the needle in an unworked section and passes the cloth across to the woman.

"I have never seen such fine stitching. Wherever did you learn such techniques?"

"My mother taught me everything I know."